A N Donaldson studied Philosophy and Economics
at New College, Oxford, before working as a
barrister in Lincoln's Inn and the City of London.
He has travelled widely in over 60 countries.
Visit his website at:
www.andonaldson.co.uk

'Necromancy, witchcraft and gruesome goings on among the dreaming spires. This historically based, well researched and beautifully written blood chiller will have you looking over your shoulder for nameless horrors. Beware of the ending, particularly if you suffer from bad dreams.'

Stella Rimington

Prospero's Mirror

A N Donaldson

&

First e-published in Great Britain by Endeavour Press Ltd 2013
This paperback edition published by A N Donaldson in
association with Endeavour Press
© A N Donaldson 2013

The right of A N Donaldson to be identified as the author
of this work has been asserted by him under the
Copyright, Design and Patent Act, 1988.

A catalogue record for this book is available from the British Library

Visit the author's website at:
www.andonaldson.co.uk

Paperback ISBN 978-0-9575879-0-8

Printed in Great Britain by Imprint Digital

For Miss F

With many thanks to Bill Hamilton for his advice &
assistance,
to TC & TM for their textual suggestions,
to AK for his technical & design support
and to my parents for everything.
Plus a special mention, as promised, for Patsy P.
And finally an apology to the shade of the great
M R J, which has caused me many troubled nights
since I so traduced his memory…
Requiescat in Pace.

Contents

Prospero's Mirror

A 'Ghost Story'

A N Donaldson

'We discovered, with the inevitability of discoveries made late at night, that mirrors have something grotesque about them.'
Jorge Luis Borges

Part 1 – Prospero's Mirror

'Spirits participate in delusion,
in the same manner as the forms in mirrors.
For that which is a perversion of being,
and deceives the mind and the senses,
is an abomination in the eyes of the Gods.'
Iamblichus' Fragment on the Mysteries

I found this in the Proceedings of the Honourable Society of Antiquaries:

'The Society will be interested to learn of an appall-
ing discovery. It concerns the scholar and medievalist
M R James. He is now more famous for writing the
greatest ghost stories in the English language. These
stories were inspired by his vast knowledge of antiquar-
ian arcana.

James managed to combine this scholarship with his
position as Provost of Eton, which he held from the First
World War until his death in 1936. His biographers tell us
his personal journals come to an abrupt halt on Novem-
ber 30th, 1935.

Yet in the archives of Old College, Oxford there have
surfaced the papers of Herbert Fisher, the then College
Warden. These papers, for many years unread, contain
the following documents. They were apparently removed
from James's effects after his death, perhaps to prevent

a scandal. The Society can thus for the first time publish the missing final pages of James's journal. They are not for the fainthearted:'

From the journal of M R James. Vol. 12:
Eton, 1935:

'December 1st

Morning

'We are each our own Devil, and we make this World our Hell.' The end of Michaelmas Half is my favourite time of year. The School is never more beautiful than now: a crisp December day over Windsor. The sun blinks through the frost on the windows at College Chapel. The early snow has settled on the roofs and on the fields, and a stiff wind blows it into drifts. The boys throw it at each other by the handful, and the breath of their laughter can everywhere be seen, hanging frozen in the winter air. Truly, no other spot in England can inspire such calm. Yet I find I cannot quite shake off the shadow of my former fears. I have written nothing for so long now: my mind is willing but my brain seems unable to obey.

The collegers have constructed a huge snowman on Luxmoore lawn. That of course is technically out of bounds. But he is such a fine specimen. I think we may allow him to stand guard there for another day or so until the Christmas vac. There is some talk that he looks like me, and indeed the mortarboard and pipe may point that way, though his girth is a little un-flattering.

Last night we made a valiant assault upon the mulled brandy punch, and a merry crowd we were too. In fact, I slept like a top, and it was rather harder than usual to get out of bed this morning. It is not terribly nice to grow old, but I suppose one must be thankful for the mercy of one's health.

But there – I have forgotten it again – the telegram. It was sitting waiting for me on my breakfast table. Late, as ever, for Chapel, I swept it up with the rest of the post.

An odd thought, that: all morning it has waited patiently, nestled in my inside jacket pocket. And there was I going happily about my normal business, quite undisturbed by any foreboding. I might have left it there and never read the thing. It was not until lunch-break, as I sat to finish the newspaper and was reaching for my glasses, that I felt the stiff corner of the envelope through my waistcoat, and remembered it.

Its contents come as something of a shock.

'CHAPMAN KILLED. I AM COMING DOWN.
I HAVE A DARK WONDER YOU MIGHT
ILLUMINATE. FISHER.'

I read it over again now. How horrible – that use of the subjunctive. But dear me, Chapman killed? Killed how, poor fellow? And why should my old friend Herbert Fisher think that, out of everyone on Earth, he should come all the way down from Oxford to see me? Chapman is a great polymath and scholar, to be sure: there were few indeed who could match his knowledge of archaeology and ontography. But as for me: I barely knew the man, beyond the occasional academic correspondence. Indeed I have not seen him in the flesh, these what – it must be seven years? – I forget.

Still, I cannot wait to renew my close friendship with Fisher. I used to see him all the time, back when he was Minister for Education, but I fear we rather lost touch when he took the Old College Wardenship. He is such a humane man, and so impressive an historian. It will be a great pleasure to speak with him again, even after such grave news. I wonder what he means by it? Here is a mystery, and no mistake: a mystery wrapped up tight in an enigma.

7

Afternoon

After break I did an odd thing I don't believe I ever did before. I was taking register for my third form Latin Grammar class. I began to read out a page from the front of my lower school register book. Michaelmas 1909. It is curious: one remembers the boys from those days much more vividly than the recent crop. A really naughty class that was, I now recall, and I was forced to be quite liberal with the birch. They suffered badly, though, when they left school, what with the War and the Influenza – their year and the year below them more than any. I *wish* I had not read out their names.

After that of course the third form were silly for the rest of the hour; though I suppose that is always the way at the end of term. But why of all pages should I have turned to that one? I fear I am losing focus more and more. The horror of forgetting everything sometimes fills my mind. I think nowadays they would say I have a complex about it.

I was quite out of sorts during entrance interviews too, or so the School Secretary said. He thinks I should revise my low opinion of them. They were queer boys, I thought. One looked like a foreigner despite his English name – he was thin and sinister, and already his upper lip is in need of a proper shave. Not at all the wholesome type that would do credit to the School. I thought to have made a good quip about 'the battle of Waterloo may have been won on the playing fields of Eton, but it seems these days we're lucky if we can scrape together a single decent cricket team'. Apparently I made the very same joke last week.

That was the final straw. I decided to ask Dr Burrows about these tiresome little slips of mine. I went over to see him at three and he gave me an examination. I suppose

I deserved his usual speech, in that soothing Lowlands brogueof his. He thinks there is no need to fear for now, but says it is time that I tried to do less: that my duties here as Provost combined with my academic researches are simply too much to bear. I must not squander 'what remains of my physical capital'. And I should avoid exciting myself, or putting too much strain upon my nerves. He also told me my other *infortuné* is not uncommon for a man of my age. We had a rather anatomical conversation, and then moved on – mercifully – to other topics.

Burrows continues to labour under the misapprehension that it is part of his duties to keep me abreast of current scientific thinking; surely a task as thankless as it is hopeless. Though it is indeed incredible what he tells me: that the part of each atom that is solid is infinitesimal even by the standards of the infinitesimal. We are empty, it seems. And particles that travel faster than thought stream through us all the time. Truly, the laws of Nature are more fantastic than all the most extravagant conceits of superstition.

Evening

Fisher arrived somewhat flustered on the four forty-five. He has gone grey, and looks older – though of course I told him otherwise. Time has, I suppose, taken much out of all our lives. He was pleased to see me, and I him, but he is in a very odd temper. He was more excited than I have ever seen him before. He had, I thought, a somewhat hunted look about him. He was perpetually glancing around him and over his shoulder. I was only half way through the usual 'Ave!' when he cut me off short with a raised hand and said, in a queer low voice:

'I think I may have been followed here.'

I asked him what he meant by that and he would say nothing. Beneath his stern Victorian features he seemed nervous and oppressed. Though in truth who would not be after such terrible news.

'What an awful thing – poor Chapman,' I said. 'What happened? Who is to blame?'

I expected to hear, perhaps, that he had been knocked over by a motorcar.

'What do you mean, Monty?' said Fisher, smoothing down his hair. 'He died in bed.'

'Your telegram said he was 'killed' . . .'

'Oh did it?' he said, looking pained, before launching into one of his characteristic sophistries: 'Well I suppose he was 'killed' – killed by a seizure – if you want to split hairs on linguistics. Either way he is dead. 'He *is* dead.' That won't do either, will it? For what sense is there in saying someone *is* – now, at this present moment of time – in a state of non-existence? Language lets us down with these things. Be that as it may his heart gave out, and he is taken from us, and there's an end on it.

'He was working too hard, and in a sense I am to blame for that. I should not have troubled you, perhaps, but it is what he was working *on*, Monty – there I believe you may render a very great service to a very old friend – that is, if you will.'

'Of course, Herbert,' I said, 'whatever service I can –'

'Would you really do it?' he blurted. He seized my arm with a painful grip and stared at me like a man possessed. 'I knew it. I knew you would.'

He was in a most peculiar state of grief, tinged – it almost seemed – with alarm. He only really revived when we were finally sat in the common room, with our feet stretched out before a roaring fire and two very large sherries in our hands. Outside the temperature had dropped again but in by the fire we were snug. For a time we stared in silence at the flames. A log settled noisily and I noticed Fisher flinch. I sensed some last reluctance that had to be overcome. Finally I ventured to ask:

'So, Herbert, what is this 'dark wonder' of yours?'

The light from the flames was reflected from the rim of his glasses, which sat perched uncertainly on the end of his aquiline nose. I saw a knot of tension in the lines around his eyes at last relax, as if he had finally made up his mind.

'Well,' he said, with a penetrating sideways look, 'you had better see for yourself!'

And that is when I first saw it.

He took it from a battered leather doctor's bag, where it was nestled carefully inside a rug. It was heavy. It was wrapped up in crisp cream paper tied with string. He now loosened this and passed it to me. He added: 'Happy Christmas, Monty,' with that mock levity of his, and a somewhat crooked smile.

It is sitting on my study desk before me as I write. It impresses me more than I could have conceived such an object might have that effect. What a magnificent piece. It is some eighteen inches high by twelve across. The setting is finely crafted, with trim bevelled edges and the original paint still showing. On the reverse: a picture – painted straight onto its wooden frame by a naïve sixteenth century hand, with iconography typical for the reign of Elizabeth I. It shows the personified figure of Britannia, whose resemblance to Good Queen Bess herself must surely have been intended. She stands in splendour in a glorious landscape. She is flanked by the kneeling figures of King Arthur and St George. They exhort her (so the caption says) to look to the sea defences that guard the Empire of Britain.

To the base – a badly scratched setting of jade scored with crude and ancient figures – there has been affixed in tarnished silver the strange 66 letter motif:

CIADSVOPFELQVIUTCRIEAMACSTORQIVUU

HOQSDAOMSDOIPNITSCRTIIRSHENLMPE!D

Finally within the frame there is the mirror itself – one great black piece of obsidian. Dark and intensely polished. Cool, surprisingly cool, to the touch. Like the inverse of a normal mirror; it almost sucks light *out* of a room. The stone is in no way so reflective as manufactured glass. It throws a passable likeness, but distorted. In fact, until you are used to it, a rather unpleasant effect. Am I really grown so old and ugly? Hardly the fairest of them all. I must send to town for new lenses; my eyesight, I fear, is now very poor. But viewed through a magnifying glass what exquisite effects: such richness, such depth and – with firelight – such *movement*.

It is enough to make one wonder why we went over to silvered glass at all. Though I should not like to shave before a shifting obsidian reflection, lest I cut my own throat. But, for all that, what it lacks in precision of detail it more than compensates in richness of image. Such thoughts come to mind when I gaze at it; such strange and vivid thoughts. The longer you stare into it the more unsettling it becomes. At last you begin to realise: there is something mesmeric to your own reflection. Something mesmeric and odd. You get the strange impression it may have just got back, having conducted some business quite different from what you have yourself been about. How stern and reproachful it is as it watches you. I wonder why I never noticed that before.

'Well Sir, where do you come from?' I asked it, for it seems to have a life of its own.

'It is brought up from the very bowels of our vaults,' says Fisher. 'Old College has plenty of dark corners. If you go poking around in them, you'd amazed what you can drag out into the light, if it wants to be found. Until last month this mirror's not been touched for nineteen years. Not since Warden Spooner got it out twenty years ago at the height of the War. Though the records of that in the archives have for some reason been redacted. Before then it seems no-one's looked into it since Eighteen Hundred and Five. Chapman managed to dig up this letter from that year. It is from Warden Samuel Gauntlett to Prime Minister Pitt.'

Here he reached in his pocket and took out a note, which he carefully passed to me. It was an elegant hand on faded thin paper. It read as follows:

'Sir,

In view of the grievous news from France we chanced the stone. The boldest of the scholars was appointed for the attempt. Thank the Good Lord the gentleman is a stout fellow. He has so far withstood the test with fortitude and resolution, though in truth we do fear greatly for his sanity. Rest assured, Sir, that the urgency of his assays will be matched by the earnest vigilance of:

your, etc etc,
SG.'

'I leave it to you,' said Fisher, 'to consider the signifi-
cance of those dates. As Napoleon said at the time: *'Let
us be masters of the Channel for six hours and we are
masters of the World'*. I need hardly tell you the worth of
such an object if it is genuine.'

'You think it an important piece?' I gasped, barely following him at all.

'That,' he said, 'is the question that I wish you to help
me answer – if you would. Chapman was working on this
for me, you see, before . . . Well I have reason to believe
he had made progress. But the areas he was looking at
were rather arcane. And it will clearly need an expert to
make head or tale of any of this. Monty, I must tell you
something he said about the extraordinary properties –'

At this he lowered his voice to a conspiratorial tone. But
just then we were interrupted by Dr Burrows, whose dour
Scottish features cracked into a smile of recognition.

'Hullo again Mr Fisher,' said Burrows, 'it has been
far too long since you last graced our humble school. I
say Monty, what have you got there? May we look at it?
*'For now we see through a glass darkly, but then face to
face'.'*

'Oh,' replied Fisher, off-hand, 'it is just something I
wanted to show Monty in order to get his opinion. Hello,
Doctor . . . do join us.'

But as Burrows went to fetch another chair, Fisher
turned to me with an urgent whisper:

'Say you will help me!' he said. 'You are the greatest expert on medieval and early modern artefacts that I
know – or trust.'

'Well this is indeed mysterious,' I said, 'But I am sure
we shall penetrate right to the heart of the matter. I should
have to know a deal more about its provenance, though,

before I could tell you much about it. When and from whom did the College acquire it?'

'We don't know,' he said. 'That is exactly what Chapman was looking at. His notes are all as he left them, if you wish to examine them. Do you think it shall be safe here, at Eton?'

An odd question, that. Although I am indeed surprised he was so willing to bring it away from the College. It might be a tremendous artefact. And yet at the same time I got the strange impression he could barely wait to be rid of it. In fact he asked me several times whether it would be safe here in the School. I suppose the thing is very valuable. But it took some time to reassure him. And I must say I was growing quite impatient, until I remembered his generosity in bringing it. He then made pains to change the subject, after muttering something strange about my being the one who 'might know what to do with it, *when the time comes*'.

I was about to ask what in God's name he meant. But then Burrows came back with the chair and the conversation moved on. I sat back and looked into the fire. Fisher seems to have taken this Chapman business very hard indeed. Either that or he is beginning to lose his marbles. Still, I can hardly say no for the sake of our friendship. And with term now come to an end I have little enough else to do with myself. I had been thinking of a walking trip in Aldeburgh or Whitminster, but I am not sure that my poor legs could stand it. At any rate now here is something else to amuse me over the vac. After all, it might be rather diverting. It shall do me good to go out into the World. And my sanctuary here, when I return for Christmas, will then feel all the more snug and secure.

I have assented. We have agreed I shall go up to Old College tomorrow morning. I shall stay with Fisher for a few days and sort through Chapman's papers. He was relieved at this, and seemed in a state of great excitement. In all it was some while before I could calm him down enough to catch up on the rest of the Oxford news.

Just then we were interrupted by various parties eager to bear me off to dinner. I pressed Fisher to join us in Hall. He could stay the night and travel up with me tomorrow. But I got the clear impression that Mrs Fisher would be far from happy with such an arrangement. And Mrs Fisher, it need hardly be said, is not a woman to be crossed on such matters (that woman is the cause, I should say the causeuse, of much annoyance to me). With that Fisher – suddenly anxious again, though now perhaps with more reason – said he must be getting back to his wife. He agreed to see me again tomorrow in Oxford. He left the mirror with me, and I put it away in my study. I spent a busy evening on the end of term arrangements, and eating my last dinner of the half. I took a little too much port, and came to bed tired and late and happy.

Yet there must always be a discordant note to disturb my harmony. On returning to my rooms I see that a huge house spider had crept into my study. It was crouched there on its sinewy legs in the middle of the carpet. I must say I have a revulsion for such creatures. Particularly when they take it upon themselves to be quite so large and quite so hairy. They put me in mind of that horrid hair on the adult human body. They seem like Nature's envoys reminding us of her hostility. An ill omen. I stood stock-still and for a minute we eyed one another without blinking. Then I went at him with a slipper, but he galloped off under my desk at a horrible speed.

I had the maid up and we shifted all the furniture. But try as we might we cannot not find the beast, and I have had to give up the search to go to bed. I daresay he is gone, but all the same, what if he has found somewhere here to hide? What if 'he' is in fact a 'she', looking for somewhere to nest? What if she decides to explore the folds of my bed linen? What are we to do then?

December 2nd

Morning

Found it hard enough to get off to sleep last night. I felt as if spiders or daddy-long-legs or rats were crawling about in the sheets. That unwelcome visitor to my study had no doubt made my skin feel more sensitive. Eventually I dropped off and slept well enough, though was somewhat restless and disturbed.

I rose at an un-Godly hour to catch the train up to Oxford. My compartment was full but I had the window seat, and the countryside was lovely in the snow. As we puffed into the station the platform was a sea of bowler hats. Stepping down into the crowd, a young boy got under my feet – and then received a maternal clip round the ear for his pains. I passed one man – a veteran, perhaps – with a face totally disfigured by burns. I hope and trust I managed not to stare. In all it was a great relief to find myself in the back of a taxicab.

My travails were not yet over, though, for I had some sort of funny turn. I simply could not understand what the driver was saying to me. And at first, when I tried to get him to repeat it, I found it for some reason almost impossible to speak. It only lasted for a moment, but it was really rather concerning.

The city itself though, swathed in bright mist, was glorious, if a little disorienting. As usual it is a labyrinth for the Cambridge man to navigate – turning corners I kept half-expecting to find myself on the Backs. And I had a curious feeling of sadness. Each time I travel somewhere nowadays I catch myself wondering: will this be the last time I see it? But enough of this incessant morbidity. In a few days I shall be back at Eton, where I can enjoy a proper rest.

Fisher was already waiting for me at the corner of Old College Lane. He was very pleased I had come. He took me on a tour of the place, which I had not seen before, and is worth a brief description.

Looking down the length of the Lane from that corner, the mute walls on either side are entirely windowless, crusted with texture, and blackened with medieval age. There facing you at the end stands the Gate Tower: said to be the oldest in Oxford, and decorated with late gothic statues. When I first saw it smoke was hanging above its chimneys and mingling insensibly with the mist. The morning winter sun – diffusing through this mist – threw silhouettes round the crenellations: in fact a rather pleasing effect. There was not a breath of wind. All was absolutely still. Then suddenly a flight of rooks, startling themselves from a battlement, squawked up in outrage and flapped off out of sight.

At this Fisher turned to me as if to say something. But then he hesitated and changed his mind, and we walked up the lane in silence. We found the great gates into the college shut and barred against us. Into their old oak mass is cut a smaller door. This stood open: a tiny breach in a great fortress of learning. The sign on the gates reads, with inscrutable hostility:

'THIS COLLEGE IS CLOSED TO VISITORS'

Fisher gestured with an outstretched hand that I should enter. I ducked my head beneath the gnarled lintel formed by the crossbeam of the gates. A single invisible strand of spider silk, spun in mysterious and industrious silence, suddenly stopped my advance. I encountered this barrier at precisely eye-height – a most unpleasant sensation. As I stepped down inside, I had to paw with disgust at my face, in an attempt to remove the thread. A fine sight I must have made. Fisher stepped in after me and waited for me to stop. Then he said:

'Welcome to Old College . . .' and he paused, declining his head and adding, with a curious emphasis, '. . . I hope you shall enjoy your stay.'

We stood for a silent moment as we surveyed his great domain. It is well into tenth week by now – the depths of the Christmas vac – and there are no undergraduates left. Indeed the College is almost entirely empty. Inside the walls the traffic noise dies suddenly away, and with it all the rude reminders of our ugly modern age. The great quad opened out in front of us, dim and glowing. The dew on the lawn was burning off, forming the mist that sat between the buildings. Through this the sun appeared as a strange white disk, pale enough to look at. Its light glinted from the stonework and the windows. There it was melting the frost, though the North faces of the roofs shall stay iced all day. There was the faint smell of a distant bonfire. We might have stepped back into a different century. The whole College seemed like an hallucination.

'What you see here was built in the late fourteenth century. It is seldom enough remembered what our original purpose was. But we 'Wykehamists' owe our existence to William of Wykeham, who endowed the foundation 'to counter the fewness of learned men, arising from epidemics and pestilences, and other miseries of the World'.'

'Pestilences,' I repeated, 'yes of course.'

'The Black Death had not just killed off half of England,' he continued, 'it had taken a terrible toll on the University. Plagues hit the Colleges very hard, of course, because of the density of the accommodation. Anyway this is Great Quad, the core of the original foundation. It has been called one of the loveliest architectural ensembles in England. What do you think?'

The heart of the College is built in perpendicular gothic, though a rather eccentric attempt has been made to classicise some of the windows. Standing under the entrance arch, with the Warden's lodgings above you, the Chapel and the Hall to the left form the north side of the quadrangle. Directly opposite to the East there is another large arch. This leads through to a second quadrangle. Or, rather, the space to which it leads is not properly speaking a quadrangle. For it is in fact the area between two wings, projecting in widening stages. At that end they have not been enclosed (except with an iron balustrade). They give out instead onto delightful gardens. It was towards these that Fisher and I now walked.

'You'll see that we are enclosed by what is left of the old city wall.'

Fisher pointed to where this blackened masonry wrapped itself round the back of the gardens. The mist lay thicker on the sunken lawns in the lee of this ancient wall. It runs right through the college, half-ruined and clad with ivy, like something from a late Caspar Friedrich. It is overlooked on one side by a decrepit timber-framed building with impossibly angled dormers. Above it all there looms, from the centre of the gardens, a huge earthen mound. This mound is thick with dark foliage, and stepped at the front, like the over-grown pyramid of some forgotten and barbarous race. As I looked at it the skeletal branches of its ash trees reached up through mauves and greys into the bleary whites and blues above.

'This artificial hill is rather curious,' I said. 'I'll bet there is a good view from the top. Is that someone up there? Oh no – forgive me – a trick of the light in the mist. But what is it doing here anyhow? A strange sort of ornamental feature for a college, wouldn't you say?'

'Yes. Pretty isn't it? They built it up over the plague pit.'

'Ah – why did I ask!'

'I am afraid so,' Fisher said cheerfully, 'and a big one too. From a forgotten epidemic of the fifteen hundreds. Though it may've been re-used in the Great Plague, which was very bad here in Oxford. It seems to have served for the general populace as well as members of College, since there are women down there too, and of course back then they weren't allowed onto the premises.'

'How is this known?' I asked, thinking what an admirable rule that was.

'We accidentally dug one or two bodies up when we took out the old silver birch. You could tell from the bones and the long hair. The gardeners were naturally rather concerned. They thought the infection might have survived – well – in fragments of flesh. We had to get an expert in from the Radcliffe Infirmary to give us the all clear.'

'Where did you take them,' I asked, 'for reburial?'

'We realised that that would be an administrative nightmare, and would have meant tearing up half of the garden, so in the end we just turned them back over again into the earth.' He paused, and added with a smile: 'Jolly good for the soil. Can you see how well our roses have come up?'

22

Grimacing at this I let him lead me round and through to the outside of the walls. Here an open gate gives onto a much larger area. It is bounded by a vast Victorian range in a somewhat ludicrous neo-gothic. These buildings project at one end in the staircase where Fisher said Chapman was found. He pointed this out hurriedly and with some awkwardness. Then we turned back with relief through a passage and into the garden quad.

'Over behind there is the bog-house,' he said, his tone changing to a mock-heroic bathos: 'We believe with some confidence that this is the oldest continuously used lavatory in Europe. Don't expect the plumbing to have improved much since the founder's day. In there is the Senior Common Room. There's Hall. And here, of course, is Chapel.'

Inside the chapel it was dark, and cold enough to see one's breath. Our footsteps echoed in the gloomy interior. There is much in there of interest. I am resolved to go round it at leisure when I have the chance to examine it properly. There look to be some good paintings and some amusingly bad stained glass. I noted several macabre carvings on the choir stalls that will repay closer attention. There is a really unnerving statue of Lazarus in the execrable modern style. And finally a splendid monument set into the wall of the South transept: a curly-haired gentleman with a Stuart beard and moustache, in deep relief, and somewhat gingerly clutching a skull.

Against the South wall is a large war memorial. Too large. They always are. I scanned the names for those I had taught. There were two at least I recognised. Three, if that was the same Harry Landscombe (I had forgotten his College). And one of them, of course, that I already knew I should find. An old wound, though still it aches. How hard it is when those we know as children are taken from us. Harder still when they are favourites. I can picture him as a young chorister as if it were yesterday.

Fisher must have seen my reaction, for he drew my attention away to a smaller memorial on the opposite wall.

'Prinz Wolrad-Friedrick zu Waldeck-Pyrmont, Freiherr Wilhelm von Sell, Erwin Beit von Speyer . . . yes quite right of you of course,' I said. 'But did you have any trouble persuading them to put up a memorial to your German students?'

'A little, but not much. They were Wykehamists, after all, whichever side they fought on. Anyway, if you'll follow me through, out here there are the cloisters . . .'

I stepped after him into an arched stone passage. It did indeed lead to the cloisters, which surround a lawn with a great black yew tree. Here we were enveloped by an even deader stillness. In deference to it he lowered his voice to almost a whisper, and continued in his old ironic tone:

'Our College ghost is supposed to live here – the 'Black Scholar'. He strides backwards round the Cloisters: all in black from head to foot. But he doesn't seem to be at home to visitors today.'

'You've only one ghost? That is a poor showing,' I said, laughing. 'At the School we claim to have at least a dozen!'

Fisher's chuckles fell off, and he said:

'I am not surprised. I've heard Eton lost a thousand in the War. And why should the angry dead haunt the places they died, rather than the places they were longing to return?'

'Yes, well, we did our duty.'

'Did we? Do you know, to be serious for a moment, I sometimes wonder if we were no better than Giles de

Rais, or Madame Voisin, or any of the most evil child-murderers in history. They only killed hundreds to commune with their demons. We sent our boys off to die by the hundreds of thousands. Could we really look them in the eye now, with everything we hear from Europe, and tell them it was worth the sacrifice?'

I turned to him in surprise, and said: 'You mustn't say such things.'

Fisher looked away and shook his head, before reverting to his former tone:

'There it is – I am sure you are right. Anyway, we believe this whole area here was originally laid out as a graveyard. A very pleasant thing to live beside! It was for victims of the St Scholastica's Day massacre – the last great eruption of violence between the City and the University. 'Town' fought 'Gown' for three days and nights, and there were dozens killed.'

'And what is that old tower there on the North side of the cloisters?' I asked him. 'From the road I felt it must be part of the chapel, but now I see that it is not. Why does it stand apart like that?'

'*That* is the old Bell Tower. It was built onto a bastion of the walls when College was founded. I believe it was to act as a watchtower. The views from up there are magnificent. In fact, if you are game, let us go up. We no longer let undergraduates in there without permission from their fellows, as I'm afraid they will keep insisting on hurling themselves off the top – a couple of cases we've had of that, over the years.

'The tower itself, of course, has a somewhat grisly past. A rather – unfortunate – episode of College history happened in there. It all had to do with John Quinbey. He was a rather sinister character: a fellow here in the sixteen sixties. He was an infamous alchemist, and perhaps worse – something like that Count Magnus of yours. He is supposed to have got up to all sorts of no good: occult diagrams, curses written in blood, the works. One of my predecessors, Warden Woodward, had the Devil of a time dealing with him. It was Woodward's memorial you were looking at, by the way, in the chapel.'

'Do you mean to say you are being serious?' I asked, 'That this fellow Quinbey was real?'

'Real? Oh yes,' he answered, and continued ironically: 'In fact, Old Jenkins has seen him. One of our night porters. If Quinbey really is 'the Black Scholar'. And the undergraduates have a tradition of running three times round the cloisters on Allhallowe'en – or is it Walpurgis Night? – which supposedly discourages him from putting in an appearance during the term. I'm surprised you hadn't heard of it, with your interests in that area.'

I laughed and said:

'I didn't have you down as a fabulist.'

'Well as you can imagine,' he chuckled, 'I implicitly trust anything Jenkins says, particularly when he's been on the strong stuff.'

He took out a monstrous bronze key and opened the door to the tower. We clambered our way up a spiral stair, which played hell on my poor legs. But eventually it emerged through a door and we came out onto the leads.

We were above the level of the mist now and could see across the whole of Oxford. The city was bathed in magnificent light. Her monuments were at first unrecognised from this unfamiliar perspective. But one by one the neighbouring landmarks aligned themselves with their images in my memory. The college spread out indistinctly below us. Its buildings were floating and ethereal, only their pinnacles picked out clearly by the Sun. A copper roof shimmered in the distance. Fisher smiled to himself and said:

'When I come up here I am reminded of what, as an Historian, I should never forget. That the Past is always underneath us – and all around us – just out of sight. Sometimes perhaps, where really old things are, that thinnest crust of the Present can break, and the vast depths of the Past will come pouring through. Fashionable people these days often hold the Past in contempt. But this college has seen six centuries of Life and Death in all their forms. I believe it has a spirit of its own, quite implacable. Please it and it will look after you all the time you are here. Cross it, and I think it may find a way of crossing you.'

The tour of the college completed, Fisher took me back to his lodgings. His wife was waiting there for us, with a somewhat haughty impatience. She insisted on kissing me on the cheek, which is a practice I cannot abide, so that one has to try one's hardest not to be seen to flinch. She was kind enough, however, to show me to a suite of rooms that are to be mine for the length of my stay. They are up on the first floor, above the gate. They include a marvellous study lined with books. It looks to be quite an impressive collection. There is little more recent than the sixties, and several quartos a great deal older than that. I look forward to making its more systematic acquaintance.

Just off this library is a small oratory with a window into the chapel. Another door leads to the bedroom. Its windows look out over the cloisters, the cloister lawn, and the Bell tower. It is a picturesque spot, although I don't quite like the yew tree on the lawn. (For there is something about yews that is nasty, damp, and foetid.) But the rooms themselves are very handsome indeed. They have clearly not been much altered in five hundred years of use.

It is Mrs Fisher's insistence that I shall be sharing them with Mr Ockham. Mr Ockham is a large tabby, who I am told is most put out if he cannot sleep on his armchair in the study. As a cat-lover I can hardly object (not that she is the sort of woman to whom one can easily object). I do not mind feline company and we have already made good friends.

Mrs Fisher and I then spent some time commiserating over Chapman. It seems he was close friends with both of them. But here she let slip something that her husband had not mentioned. She claimed those that found his body said he had barricaded himself into his rooms. This made no sense at all to anyone. But the two Doctors who examined him called it a classic case of heart failure, and he had a long-standing cardiac weakness.

We took lunch in the Fisher's private dining room in the Lodge. We were joined by the College Chaplain, Reverend Simmons. He is a great friend of theirs. I could well understand why, for he is rather a charming character. He combines shortness and plumpness almost to the point of sphericality. His face is a soft pudding of laughter-lines, close-shaved cheeks, and a very smooth, fat neck, which bulges out alarmingly between his chins and his clerical collar. He has a cheerful, disarming manner, and a tendency against the serious, which I suspect disguises a rather unusual intelligence. Mrs Fisher warned me that his wife is an invalid, who never goes out. He cares for her at home, which I think is a wonderful thing.

Simmons is – or at least pretends to be – a great fan of my old ghost stories. On these I was cross-examined closely, both on detail and on theory. I used to find such conversations tiresome. But this one was actually rather flattering. I had made some comment about the horrid possibility that of all things it would be them for which I am remembered, when I am gone.

'Nonsense,' Simmons said, 'but they deserve to be remembered: poor Dennistoun, who thinks he's pulled a fast one, when he buys that illuminated manuscript for a song, only to realise too late that there is a demon that comes with it. Or my other favourite (what do you call it?), with the teacher and his Byzantine coin, who ends up drowned down a well, clasped tight by the corpse that had dragged him there. Don't you see? You have given us the reticent tale of terror. And shown how much worse that is than horror and gore. Sure there is a place for Poe, and his grotesque baroque canvases. But they won't keep a man awake like a subtle sketch from James.'

'Why that is a contest I should very much like to see,' said Fisher. 'No offence intended, but my money is on Poe.'

'Charmed, I am sure!' I said.

'Ignore him,' said Simmons, 'he is being wicked on purpose. Your technique is the superior. Poe spreads the butter too thick. But tell me, if you would: what are your rules?'

'Too kind, Reverend, I am not sure that is true. And as for *rules*, I do not really know. I would only say, I suppose, that one should never fully show . . . never fully explain . . . and *never* moralise: I have no time for bad men or good ghosts. One should not have more than one supernaturalism at once . . . And I find I prefer stories which preserve an ambiguity.'

'Like your namesake veers at in 'Turn of the Screw'?'

'I met him once – he talked like a respectable butler. But yes if you will. One must come at oblique things obliquely. And one more thing: I prefer a nasty end. Your victim may contrive a Christian burial for the body, but that alone should never lay the ghost.'

'And what do you think will be the impact of the cinematograph? Do you enjoy it?'

'Oh dear me, no! I cannot see what it can possibly add. In any case, ghost stories are really for the young. You realise that when you get to my age. Time and all its horrors are far worse than any story . . . but let us not speak of them.'

'You raise an interesting question,' said Fisher, joining in: 'We know there are no such thing as ghosts, so why are we all scared of them? And why do we enjoy stories about them? Is it to do with our hopes of an afterlife? Or are they a sort of catharsis – a metaphor for our fear of Death?'

'No thinking, gentlemen, please!' I said, 'I am a humble schoolman now. I can no longer keep up with you young university bucks.'

'Or perhaps,' said Simmons, laughing, 'it's because we suspect there's something in them. Maybe some places can be indeed be bad, and some innocent-seeming objects very dangerous: a doll's house, a mezzotint, even an old book. Your scholarly heroes pry, only to wish they hadn't. For me your stories show how thin is our veneer of 'reason'. Behind the elegant Queen Anne façade, there always lies the gothic mansion. But tell me: why so many haunted houses and never a haunted College?'

'I never thought of that.'

'Our cloisters here are haunted, did you know?'

'Oh really, Reverend,' said Fisher, 'that is nothing but College nonsense, as you know – a joke amongst the undergraduates.'

'That is not quite what I heard,' said Simmons with a shrug, in a tone that was conciliatory, but not consenting.

After lunch Simmons took his leave. Fisher apologised for him. He thinks his spiritual beliefs are a product of his wife's condition, and his hopes that some part of her might go (or already be gone) to a better place. Fisher says this is nonsense: that the Dead are gone, and are nothing, and that nothing is left behind. For me, though, that thought is if anything more terrible.

'He must have been speaking to our night porter,' he said. 'Jenkins is the repository of College folklore. I have heard him describe the 'Black Scholar' several times, and each time the story has got worse. Real 'Raw Head and Bloody Bones' when he has had a few. I fear what really afflicts that man is not bodiless spirits but distilled ones. (But who can begrudge a drink to a man who was half-crippled fighting for his country?) For myself, I shall never believe it. Unless a ghost can wield a crowbar. For it is one of those that must have prised open the door to the Bell tower last week. It was of no great moment. They couldn't break into the treasury chests, whoever they were, and it seems they left empty-handed.'

Then Fisher did something odd. He asked after the mirror. And when I told him I had it safe in my trunk he looked shocked, and then he said something like:

'What? You mean to say you have brought the blessed thing back?'

I explained that I would naturally need it with me whilst I went through Chapman's notes, if I was to have any hope of getting to the bottom of exactly what it was.

31

'Yes of course,' he said, 'quite so, quite so. I just thought . . . well, there it is. I would be grateful if you could keep that to yourself. And keep it here in the lodge, will you? That's where we put it when Chapman was here. As I said, there have been some break-ins around the College. And there has been rather too much interest in this object already. There's a Latvian-German chap here, a fellow called Schwarzgruber –'

'Professor-Doctor Schwarzgruber?'

'Yes, why, do you know him? He's up on sabbatical from Heidelberg. A nasty little piece of work too, if you want my opinion. He's been badgering me to let him have it for weeks, though, God alone knows why. In fact it was his sudden passion to borrow it that prompted me to look into it in the first place. That is why I called in Chapman.'

This is a real surprise and pleasure. For although Fisher may not know it, in some academic circles Schwarzgruber is now rated as one of Europe's most impressive historians of the occult. I have read several of his papers with great interest (I remember his theories on the Voynich manuscripts were amusingly macabre). And next to Fitzpatrick at Cambridge and Montague Rhodes James (though perhaps here I flatter myself), he must know more about the Western esoteric tradition than any man alive. I have long wished for the chance to lock horns with him.

'Schwarzgruber is here?' I said. 'That is excellent news. I can't imagine why you called in Chapman. Not when you had someone of Schwarzgruber's stature right here under your nose. I have never met him myself, but I certainly know him by reputation. He did some outstanding work on the Tübingen Alchemists –'

'Well, that's as may be. But old Warden Spooner once told me this mirror was vital to the College. I want to know what it is before I just lend it out to anyone. Particularly a foreigner like Schwarzgruber. Particularly at a time like this. For I fear something terrible is coming . . .'

At this he unburdened himself about the state of the College and, indeed, of the Nation. He raved against a party of reformers who oppose him at every turn. He believes that several of the fellows now lean toward Moscow. I refuse to believe it. Though it is true I had rather be in Eton than at Oxbridge nowadays. I am shocked to see this place seems positively to be overrun with Marxists, atheists, and – which is worse – women.

He is also incandescent about international affairs. He says that Hoare shall have to resign as Foreign Secretary for his craven concessions to the Italians over Abyssinia. Fisher for one will be pleased to see him leave the Government: for though he is an Old College man, when it comes to the conference table he has 'a tendency to live up to his name'.

In all he seems convinced that there will be another war. He says that this time we have done nothing to prepare ourselves; and that Civilisation itself is at stake. We must all of us, even the old men, be prepared to lay down our lives. Must we really? I think I should rather die at home in my bed.

'Progress is not a law of nature,' Fisher said. 'The ground gained by one generation may be lost by the next. The thoughts of men may flow into channels which lead to disaster . . . even to barbarism.'

'Let us not think about it,' I said.

'Not think about it! What else can one think about? That the War might after all have been for *nothing*. That

33

is something for us all to think about. A true horror. Don't you realise that an insane Germanic racialism threatens our entire way of life? If we do not act soon we may yet squander our humanity, our toleration, and our good sense. And our Christian ethics may be replaced by a disgusting Nordic paganism.'

There was more in this rhetorical vein, as if he were still stood at the dispatch box. Then he muttered something obscure about:

'It seems others before me have thought this – that next time guarding the coast from invasion will not just be a matter of building beacons, Martello towers, pill boxes, and the like. Who knows? – perhaps it never was.'

He alluded to 'contacts' of his who are talking re-armament. He was a minister of state, of course, and is still well connected in London. So perhaps he knows more of this than what we read of in the papers, which I suppose is grim enough. I tried hard to get him off the topic, asking him about the college and so on. But of course he would keep coming back to 'the beastly Hun'. Finally I made some comment in a spirit of diplomacy. I said nothing would ever wash them clean of what they did to Reims cathedral. Far from calming him down this caused a nasty explosion. He said (and I shall find it hard to forget it):

'Sometimes, Monty, I wonder if you have any inner life at all. You won't just be able to keep yourself wrapped up in your books, like you did in the last show. They'll come over here, you know – Eton will be crawling with them.'

At this he sensed he had crossed the line, and added some soothing apologies. But the barb still struck. He cannot be right of course. The civilised nations all know that another War would be dreadful. The thought of my wonderful boys going off again to fight really is too much to bear. But then what do I know? More and more of late I feel the World has changed and I no longer understand it. I must console myself that *'if much is taken, much abides'*. But to listen to Fisher we must expect our Empire will be lost, our boys sent off again to die, and all that is old and beautiful blown away forever. I will not believe it.

Afternoon

Fisher took me to Chapman's rooms to show me his papers. We walked over to staircase thirteen – which is a rather desolate building they nickname 'Pandemonium'. It is formed by the projecting wing of the neogothic range and is, Fisher says, completely empty in the vac. Chapman's set is on the top floor. It faces south out over the College towards the city wall and the Mound. His desk is up against a trefoiled bay window, somewhat obscured by ivy. What thin sunlight that managed to force itself through revealed great screes of paperwork strewn around the floor. These are in quite some state of disarray. Almost as if Chapman had been shifting anxiously through them. Or perhaps the scout disordered them, when she did the room, after it happened. Though apparently he is – I should say was – one of those types to whom tidiness did not come naturally. Fisher joked grimly that 'it was one of the great mysteries of nature, but Chaps always had such an ordered mind'.

On the right was another door through to a tiny room (with an even smaller window). This was empty except for a basin, a chest of drawers, and a bed. It would have been there, I suppose, that they found the poor fellow, two days ago. Not an entirely pleasant thought, that, as Fisher bade me farewell, and I sat down with my back to the room to make a start on his papers. From the window I watched him crossing the quad below me and disappearing back to his lodge. I wondered what he had meant, when he had joked on the way up the stairs, that 'Pandy' had a bad reputation. Presumably no more than that those undergraduates who live here during term have a penchant for rowdyism.

Be that as it may, now I at last had the pleasure of examining Chapman's papers. I was eager to see what he had discovered. I began to sift them carefully. They are extremely obscure, confused, and fragmentary. There are great piles of paperwork, and I immediately notice several books on witchcraft. One does not lightly meddle with such matters. Here are pages of notes with magical lettering. But I cannot read them without laborious translation. Even those parts Chapman has translated make no sense to me:

'A stronger Power shall require a stronger summons.'

'The seven keys must not be spoken.'

'Five times he calls him and five times he turns away.'

Well that is typical of the obfuscation you find in grimoires and other magic books. But what the Devil is this, scrawled deep into the paper and written over many times, then circled? -

$$\diagup \; \daleth \; \mathcal{E} \; \mathcal{L} \; \cancel{\times} \; \cancel{\gimel} \; \bigvee$$

Or (to give those hermetic letters their English names):

'*Gisg Graupha Xtall Med Orh Und Pa*'

Suddenly I feel that there is something slightly wrong with the room. Perhaps it is the shape of it. If proportions can be harmonious they can also be indefinably repulsive. Or possibly it is a quality of the light? A cheerless glow from a sickly yellow bulb. No – that's it! – it is a noise. A very high-pitched noise, barely audible – more of a pressure than anything else – that I sense or seem to sense in one ear, and which then gets higher and higher until it fades out into infinity. I feel it several times throughout the day. I cannot make my up mind whether the phenomenon is internal or real (though perhaps that is not a distinction that makes any sense). Or it may be my poor hearing deteriorating again: these days I am plagued with all sorts of buzzes and murmurings.

It seems from his notes that Chapman shared my suspicions of what this object might be. But we will need a deal more proof before we can allow ourselves such a dark and exciting conclusion. He had not de-ciphered, at any rate, the coded message attached to its front. For his notes show he abandoned that attempt right at the start. What else they show will be harder to discover. I fear it will be no simple job to find what progress, if any, he had made.

The first step is to establish the provenance of the thing. On this Chapman has left some oblique descriptions of the fruits of his labours. He had started by looking at the notes of one Sampson, former professor of history and archivist at the College. It seemed he was the last person to have had anything to do with the object. He had left it in the College Treasury where Fisher had recently found it. Sampson's papers were mostly dated from late May of 1916. They were indeed curiously full of redactions. So many redactions that it was probably impossible to get any real sense from them at all. Amongst them there was also a note from December 1918. It was written to the then Warden Spooner. It stated in terms that the 'End of All Wars' was 'a good time to cover these unpleasant tracks for ever'. Was this Sampson still around, perhaps, to give some explanation of what he had meant? No – here was an obituary notice Chapman had dug out of the College Gazette:

'January, 1919. The College remembers Edward Sampson MA (Cantab), DPhil (Oxon), who died peacefully in his bed in College. He was 58.'

Were there, perhaps, any earlier references? There was the letter from Gauntlett to Pitt, which Fisher had already shown me, but which still made no sense at all. Before that, it seemed there was no mention of the thing. Excepting perhaps for an entry in an inventory of college treasures and plate of 1759. That was highly ambiguous. But – at a pinch – it might just have referred to the same object. Then at last I saw a note in a page of Chapman's scrapbook. It was in the bottom corner and he had ringed in pencil: N.21. BB. Arch: W/1665.12.

I spent an hour or so putting his papers back into some order. (For really, it did almost seem as if they had been deliberately ransacked.) Finding nothing much else of use, I concluded this would be the best place to start.

Making my way down 'Pandemonium' staircase, I heard a door open somewhere above me. So Fisher must have been wrong to say that the rest of the building is empty. Or perhaps it was simply an echo.

I returned to the lodge to ask Fisher where I might consult the College archives. The part-time College archivist, to whom I was shortly introduced, is a tiny, wrinkled little man who resembles nothing so much as a walnut. When I showed him the reference he knew immediately what I was asking for:

38

'Ah so you have found it too,' he said, in a reedy, nervous voice: 'The nasty secret in the College archives. Professor Chapman was asking after that only the other week. I don't know why he wanted to look at it, but it makes for absorbing reading, albeit rather gruesome. Yes I have the copy I made for him somewhere here – he brought it back a few days ago. He was rather anxious that no-one else should see it . . . Well I suppose if you have permission from the Warden . . .'

Like all archivists and librarians, he made it abundantly clear how annoying it was of anyone to have the effrontery to wish to get something down to read. He looked put out and said:

'It will take me a few minutes to find it. These archives are very extensive, you know.'

I told him with some relish that, back when I was a proper academic, I had personally catalogued all the Cambridge College archives. I would be more than happy to wait.

With that the man scurried off into a back room. From there I could hear the exaggerated sounds of his deliberately laboured searches. But the rest of the archives were left at my mercy. They were in a typical state of disorder, but I decided to have a brief poke around. I doubted it would take too long to find what I wanted. It only took a few minutes of digging to find it.

It turned out to be a letter from young Fanshawe to his tutor, dated February 1915. He was writing to explain his decision to postpone his Mod.'s in order to sign up. 'I love it here', he had written, 'and whatever happens I shall make sure to return.' Apart from that there was only a card, sent from his regimental HQ. It recorded (in matter-of-fact tone) his death, a few weeks later, outside

Bellewaarde. Well there it is. An old wound, as I say. And I am not sure there is anything more to add.

Eventually the archivist reappeared clutching a sheaf of papers. He grudgingly consented to let me take them away with me. I immediately took them back to the lodge. Here I settled down in a comfortable chair in the study, with a blanket over my knees, a pipe in my hand, and Mr Ockham snuffling to himself by the fire. Only then did I allow myself to start reading them. And very curious they were too. They must be the darkest thing I have read for many a year. I think the best thing is simply for me to set out the relevant parts of the copy in full:

Part 2 – The Invisible College

'A blight is on our harvest in the fields,
A blight is on our grazing flocks and herds,
A blight is on our womenfolk in labour;
And armed with brazen torch the God of Plague
Hath swooped upon our city to empty
Her while feeding full the sickly realm of Hell.'
Oedipus Tyrannos

'The Reflections and Admonitions of Michael Woodward, of the Old College of St Mary of Winchester in Oxford, Warden. For the Illumination of my Successors, when I am dead, that they may recognise the Sure Signs of Witchcraft that did lately and most terribly afflict our College.

The Plague came from the East. It erupt'd, it is said, in India and Coromandel, where it destroy'd a prodigious Multitude of the Mohammedans and Hindoostanis of that Countrie, who do blaspheme God and worshippe Deviles. The Tidings of its Devastations were brought to Christian Lands by Shippes of the Dutch Compagnie, which sail'd from Chinsura and Ceylon; but they did sail too late, for

41

the Distemper was already amongst them, as it seems, and when they arrived into the Portes and Harbours of Holland they had hoist the black Flag, being as they were a Pest Fleet, and bearing with them the very Evil the News of which they had come to report. And so it was, throughout the year of Our Lord Sixteen Hundred and Sixty Four, that the most dreadful Plague of Pestilence raged mightily amongst the Dutch, both at Sea and on the Land, to punish them for their manifold Impieties.

In Oxford life continued unawares, the University Men and the Townsfolk being given fully up, as they had been since the Death of My Lord the Lord Protector, to Licence and Debaucherie and to vain brutish Pleasures. The Tavernes and the Stews were all open and much patronised, even by our own Fellows, whose ill Discipline and naughtie and intemperate Behaviour were woeful to behold. But little did we then guess, that the most Diabolick Crimes against Almighty God were being carried on in our very Midst, and amongst our own Fellowship, even here in the College.

My Suspicions of Mr Quinbey first began at Christmastide that Year, at the Time of the Appearance of that dreadful hairy Comet, or fallen Star, which our Clergymen all declared was Harbinger of grievous Calamity, War, Pestilence, and Death to the Realm, as indeed turn'd out to be the Truth.

He was most melancholick of Temper, and exceeding odd in his Habits and Apparel, being tall and thin with an unkempt Wig, and having Eyes which stared unblinking, or look'd this way and that as if distract'd, so that it appear'd he cared but little for his Interlocutors, and indeed held all of us in the highest Contempt. He had a curious Manner of speaking, too, besides his Huntingdonshire Accent, so that he would hum and twitch and repeat himself, and was ofttimes seen walking alone around the Cloister, muttering like a Man possess'd. His Temper was infamous, and there had been great Disturbance the Year before, when he had attack'd and beaten one of the Servants who, he said, had upset his Instruments when readying his Room.

He was said to have extraordinary Powers of Logick and Mathematicks. He was a Favourite amongst the saucy Undergraduate Fellows, who would take him to Tavernes and ask him to perform amazing Feats of Memory and Calculation, for which he achieved a sort of Fame amongst them, as having Powers of Recall that were nothing short of miraculous, or – I should rather say – unnatural. For it was said he could be shown three disorder'd Sets of gaming Cards, and recount without Mistake the compleat Order of them, in which they were placed betwixt one another, which is indeed a Thing to be wonder'd at.

He appear'd never at Chapel, and but seldom at Hall. He ate sparingly, and ofttimes he had forgot to eat at all, so that it were hard enough to see how he continued alive, and indeed he was terribly thin and pale. He slept but little, continuing his Studies until Three o'Clock of the Morning, and then prowling about the College, wrapt in a long black Cloak.

Of the Nature of the diabolical Studies which occupy'd these unnatural Hours he kept, the first we knew was when some of the Fellows complain'd of an unholy Stink, that seem'd to come from Quinbey's Rooms, and it was discover'd he was keeping diverse Vessels of his own liquid Excreta. From this it was believed he was attempting to distil Gold, although he did violently deny it, claiming rather his Great Work was the creating of a baser

Substance, that he call'd Luciferium, for it burn'd cold, and threw an awful and unnatural Light. He was call'd before the Fellows and reprimand'd, it being against the Law of the Realm to conduct these alchemical Experiments, besides his Methods were most noisome and unsavoury, and he did desist.

He had took instead to standing out a'Nights upon the Mound, notwithstanding the great Frost that there then was, observing the Progression of that terrible Star across the Heavens, which had come to rise betimes, and to make a great Arch, and had gone quite to a new place in the Sky than it was in before, so that it hung malignant above the Citie, 'incumbent on the dusky Ayre', a harbinger of God knows what Disaster. An horrid thing it was to be sure, and great was the Feare amongst the Townsfolk of what it did portend. Yet Quinbey seem'd bewitch'd with it. The Bursar told me he had gone out and spoken with him, and call'd it an horrid Thing, and that Quinbey had said that rather it was most beautiful, and that he should not speak of its Appearance who had not seen it closer to, as he himself had the Night previous, and that he believed its Arrival would change the World, which was a most curious Way of speaking.

On Our Lord's Day, or Christmas Day, I did dine in Hall, with twenty Fellows with me, and a very handsome Dinner we had too, with Cods boil'd, with fried Soles round them, and Oyster Sauce, a fine Sirloin of Beef roast'd, some Pease Soup and an Orange Pudding (for the first part); and (for the second) a Lease of wild Ducks roast'd, a Fore-quarter of Lamb, a Rabbit apiece (the junior Fellows Half a one each) and Salad, and minced Pies; and after the second Part there was a fine Plum Cake brought to the senior Table as is usual on that Day, which goes also to the Bachelors after. Wine went round too, that Domus pays for, and we did all drink, wishing one another Omnibus Wickhamisis and a merry Christmas. And a merry Companie it was as I recall, excepting only that my new wig did itch me, and that I was certain one of the Fishes was bad and so I sent it back.

It was in the midst of this Dinner that I ask'd Quinbey wherefore he was so desirous of watching the Comet, which all good Christians were agreed to be a woeful Apparition.

'Then,' says he, 'all 'good Christians' are as foolish as our Natural Philosophers, who hold it to be an Exhalation of the Ether betwixt us and the Moon, when it is noe such Object below the Moon, but a marvellous celestial Bodie above it, and which will prove a Prodigie for Man.'

This Outburst caused much disquiet in the Hall, and all Eyes turn'd to me to make Riposte:

'Do you mean to say, Sir, that you are one as holds with the heretical Errors of Aristarchus? You surely do not dare to contradict the written Word of God?'

'Warden,' came Quinbey's impudent reply, 'our Peace and Stillenesse are but Illusion. We stand on one of many lost Planets plummeting through boundless Space. The Revolutions of the Spheres are as quite indifferent to our Wishes as are all the secret and capricious Whims of Nature.'

'Come Sir,' says I, with I confess some heat. 'The Truth has been reveal'd to us by Holy Scriptures, fix'd in our minds by the writings of Aristotle, and confirm'd by the infallible Evidence of our own Eyes.'

'Our Eyes,' he said, with a contemptuous Laugh, 'and what of our Eyes? What indeed of our minds? Can they not both be deceived by a Mighty and Malicious Demon of the utmost Power and Cunning who, so say the French Philosophers, can confound us at every turn? Is He indeed our Friend, this Devile, who allows us to wallow content in our Mistakes, and hides from us the true Nature of the World and of Ourselves, which we could hardly bear? Or is he our grievous Enemie after all, who holds us back from being what we could be?'

This Comment seem'd to me most atheistical, and I resolved to enquire further after him around the College. I feare 'tis true that more and more of the young Fellows turn against the learning of the Schools, though with his odd manner he had but few Friends even amongst them. It seem'd he was seen to keep odd Companie about the town, where he was oft observed to meet with a Group of strange Fellows, twelve Others, some of the University and Others come up from Elsewhere, so that mark you with him they made Thirteen, though what were the Subjects of their Discourse, nobodie was able to discover, since they went to great Lengths to keep their Meetings private and their Discussions secret.

Meanwhile there were rumours that the Plague was now in London. Two Huguenots, they whisper'd, lately come with Cloth from Flanders, were dead in St Giles Parish in the Rookery with the awful Signs upon their Bodies, the Infection having been carry'd over in their Wares. For Weeks there was mighty Talk of it. All Ears strain'd for News come up from Town, though at first with little enough Fuel to feed the Fire of Gossip, but by slow Degrees the Thing began to shew itself.

By June there were in London many Hundreds dead each week, and by August 'twas many Thousands. His Majesty the King left Westminster for Hampton's Court, where they say he does indulge himself with the debauch'd

Members of his Circle, and the Afflictions of his Countrie that his Sins bring down upon us do trouble him but little, so that it might as well be said we have no Government. Word got about in London, where the Plague grew violent hot, that Oxford was a cool Bastion of safety, and many men from Parliament came hither. Those that could flee London to the Countrie did so, and the Distemper ofttimes follow'd in their Wake, for some it seem'd carried it in secret and infect'd those who welcomed them, though none could say whether they did so unknowing, or rather intend'd it. In the Countrie there was a grievous Murrain of Animals and Cattle, and even the Birds began to die, so that the very Earth itself seem'd sicke.

By Autumn this mighty Plague of Pestilence had spread with irresistible Fury across the Realm. And yet the Magistrates and Aldermen of Oxford still did Nothing, such as preventing the Ingress of countrie Folk into the Town, or putting by Stocks of Food, such as they had done during the late Siege, it being as if the Citie, invest'd as it were rather by an invisible than a tangible Foe, were incapable of knowing what Precautions it could take to save itself. Nor did the lascivious and wanton Behaviour of the Populace abate, nay rather it increas'd, so that the Manners of the People were debauch'd, and the Citie given over to Filth and Sin. It seem'd 'twas easier to deny the Thing we all fear'd than ride out to meet it, Eye to Eye.

Soon our great Commonwealth of Wisdom and Learning was wash'd about by a raging Sea of Darkenesse. One by one the Villages in the County were infect'd in a great Arc around Oxford, or rather like an ever-tightening Noose about our Citie. Some indeed were entirely desert'd, and the Folk who flood'd into Town, with terrible Stories of the Evil and Ruine that they fled, began to say they did not think there could be many left alive behind them.

It was about this Time that the seeds of my Suspicions of John Quinbey, that were plant'd last Christmastide, first took Shape and grew. He was found to be purchasing large Quantities of Tin, Copper, Quicksilver, Salt, and Ratsbane, and other divers Substances, which arous'd the Suspicion he was again bent on conducting alchemical Investigations, but the exact Nature of these were a Mystery, for he would let Nobodie into his Chambers, nor ever discuss his Work with the other Fellows.

Of greater Concern than this, he now claim'd to be deep in Catoptrics – the Study of reflect'd Light – to which End and Purpose he had purchased many Mirrors. Amongst these he had bought, from one Bartholomeus van Rijn, the 'Magickal' Looking-Glasse they say did once belong to Sir Francis Bacon, which he proudly shew'd to diverse Men. 'Tis a curious Mirror of Obsidian, no doubt used in toilet by an ancient Race. I have since conceived a sort of Fascination for it as something numinous, and spent many restless Hours in its Companie.

With it came a hand-copied Book, that call'd itself the 'Liber Mysteriorum Sextus', that purport'd to be writ by Doctor Dee, who first was given the Mirror by her Majesty Gloriana (or Queen Elizabeth), who herself received it of Sir Francis Drake when it was brought up out of Spain by the Fleet. Now I have heard it said that that good Doctor was deep in the lore of the Grimoire, and an Invocator or Caller of Devilles and the Spirits of the Dead, and that his Books were Works of Darkenesse. I hold this to be manifest Nonsense, for that he was a wise and learned Man and a good Christian could not be clearer from the many pious Sentiments he writes in this 'Sixth Book of Mystery', in which he tells how by obscure and ancient Arts he sought only to discover in this Mirror the secret Truths of God.

Yet 'tis true the *Liber Sextus* troubled me. For though most of it is writ in English, there are later Passages in another Tongue, which is no normal Language, and which I could not back at that Time read (and which I have later come to think were rather Quinbey's Work than Dee's). And the Parts of it that could be read were troubling enough. For in them Dee reports many weird Rappings and Knockings on his Table of Practice (for such he call'd the Bench on which he used the Mirror), and elsewhere in the House, and of strange lights, and of a dread Voice that spake, though not in Words, but rather 'like the Schrich of an Owl, but more longly drawn and more softly'.

He then claims that Spirits not only show'd themselves *in Crystallo*, but sometimes even step'd out and moved about the Room! He reports a Fire that broke out in his Servants' Chambers in the Night, and also that several of the Inmates of his House were Suicides, which indeed I had read elsewhere. These things would be wondrous indeed, were they but true. They say, though, that he was mislead by Swindlers and Mountebanks. But that these Men should severally have trick'd him, and should severally have claim'd (to his Terror), to have been visit'd by evil Spirits, seems curious indeed. Was it not possible that he had rather been the Victim of an *infernal* Illuder?

I myself have sought to learn strange Marvels from the Stone, though never yet have I done so, nor could I undertake those awful Rites which, I later discover'd, those coded Passages of the Book do counsel must be perform'd, by he who wants to gain safe Power over the Stone. This is too far from Christian Practice, too like the Form of Necromancie, and I will not believe that the Powers of Heaven require it or allow it. Nor can I help but suspect, though of course he would deny all, that Quinbey wrote these awful Lines himself, and that he had no like Qualms.

Accordingly we had both Book and Mirror confiscated, the Bursar insisting that it was an apt Treasure for the College, and re-imbursing Quinbey from the Funds. He was enraged at this, but on this all the Fellows support'd us, and he could think of no good Reason why we should not have it off him, unless it was indeed that he was up to no Good with it, which now I am quite sure was so.

Quinbey, lastly, now turn'd his Interest to the Corpses of Animals. These he did cut up most fearfully, as was report'd to me by the Porter, who complain'd of it, that he did make him dispose of diverse Bodies of Animals, and Parts of Animals. In particular it seem'd he was making a Study of their Eyes, so that many of the poore dismember'd Creatures he had the Porter clear away no longer had their Eyes, these being removed.

Matthew, the Butler's Boy, even told me that another Servant, whose Brother was a Gravedigger in St Aldates, did hear a Story of another of his Profession, that Quinbey had enquired after the purchase of human Cadavers, and especially of the Bodie of that Girl that was due to be hang'd last Year for Witchcraft. It was said she had kill'd her Baby (which was true), and that she had nightly Congress with a Deville, that had signed her Name with her menstrual Blood in Luciferge's Book of Death (which Foolishness I hardly can believe!). In the end Quinbey did not get her Bodie, for she was taken to the Stake up by the Castle.

I remember the Case well enough, for I witness'd the Execution myself, and the Sight of it was fired onto my Brain: even when I shut my Eyes against it, I could still see her, burning. And I later dream'd that she came to me, and enticed me amorously into Chapel, where I stripp'd and ravish'd her without Pitie upon the Altar, and committed other such wanton, gross, and filthie Deeds; at which Rats, Toads, and Salamanders crawl'd up to her to suck, and I saw she had many Teats, and she scream'd at me as she had scream'd upon the Stake. And I was then suffer'd to see the most dreadful Visions I have ever seen, of a blast'd and infernal Plain, shroud'd in a fatal Stench, on which things like Men with leather Faces threw Streams of liquid Fire at one another, under a smoke-blacken'd Sun, and the Dead lay crawling all around. I took these Dreams to be no less than a Warning of the Wages of Sins such as hers, and ever since have tried to live as well as any Christian should, and to abstain from carnal Lusts.

Finally, one Day I was summon'd to Quinbey's Chambers by a Servant, who said there was great Mischief afoot, and bid me hurry, and arriving I beheld a Commotion, for an old Laundry-woman most hysterical was there, begging several Fellows to come to her aid for the Love of God. And they, having forced open his Door, did discover Bombastus, the College Cat, tied down on its Back to a Bench by leather Straps, with its little Legs bound also, and wound'd along its Stomack most pitiably and screaming, and indeed when I first heard it I thought it was a Child. Quinbey, unperterb'd, had cut it open with a Knife, and forced his Hand inside it and ripp'd out its Spleen, which he was holding aloft in his Hands as I arrived, and laughing at them that did remonstrate with him, that no Harme would befall the Creature from this, as he term'd it, 'Experiment'. And indeed, having briefly sew'd the Creature up he let it go, and it lives still to this Day, though none can tell how (for none can catch it), and it is grown wild and will not submit to being stroked by me, though previously 'twas most affectionat.

At this I thought to have him expell'd. But my Power in the College is but poore since the return of those Fellows from Exile, and the Banishment of the Fellows who did elect me under the Authoritie of the Lord Protector, it being openly said, that I was thus little better than my predecessor, Warden Marshall, who was intrud'd by the Parliamentary Commissioners, and this most resent'd amongst the Fellowship, who did come to Quinbey's Protection (whose Father was a Gentleman Cavalier of the late King) as being one of their own.

Indeed throughout these Disturbances and what follow'd his Case became, for them, the Proxy of their Resentment at my Authoritie, so that there was but little I could do. I resolved to keep close Eye on him, that I might catch him at some further Diabolical Activity, which would quell even their Arguments that did support him. But by then there was great Distraction for God preserve us the Plague at last was come into the Towne.'

Part 3 – An Account of Some Curious Disturbances in Holywell Street

'If evil spirits perceive they are connected with
* Man . . .*
and can flow in to the things of his body,
they will attempt by a thousand means to destroy
* him;*
for they hate him with a fatal hatred.'

Arcana Celestia

Evening

My delight at the discovery of this curious document need hardly be described. The rest of it, it seemed, was going to be a catalogue of the horrors of the plague, as it entered and ravaged the city. I put that aside to read in my own time for pleasure.

My hopes, though, of its importance to my search had not been disappointed. Chapman's reference was well worth the following up. For here was as clear a piece of evidence as one could wish for: proof of the provenance and authenticity the artefact. If I had my suspicions of what it was these are confirmed. For I now see – as Chapman must have seen – it is an object of extreme age, rarity, and value.

What a pity the book of practice does not seem to have survived with it. No copies of it are known to have been made; and this missing work would have been a great addition to scholarship. Still, my decision to take up Fisher's invitation will not be a matter for regret. It is an extraordinary find. It was in a state of some excitement that I put away the archive and went, as arranged, to join Fisher for dinner in hall. I was confident he would be as pleased as I was with my progress.

I came into hall a little late. I found it pleasingly festooned with Christmas decorations. I took my place at high table, with Fisher and the few remaining fellows around me. We were somewhat huddled in the otherwise-empty space. When all were gathered Fisher proposed a toast: 'to those less fortunate than ourselves', at which we had to raise a glass to those 'poor souls at Cambridge'.

Also present were Simmons and – to my delight – Schwarzgruber. In life he is a rather peculiar little man, with a very punctilious manner. He is short and rather thin, with piercing grey eyes. He smells powerfully of carbolic soap. I can barely wait to discuss our many shared fields of interest. Perhaps this may yet bring the progress that eludes me. He spoke to me at some length about his recent excavations of the old stone circles at Uppsala, where he has found evidence of human sacrifice. He believes he will quite upset the consensus on Dark Age culture in the Baltic.

Schwarzgruber then asked what I was working on and I explained the reason for my visit. We proceeded to have one of the most intriguing conversations I have had these several years. I shall make myself record it here in detail:

'So you really think it is original?' asked Schwarzgruber, and I could see he was flushed with excitement.

I said I could confirm that it is, and that it was brought into the College by John Quinbey.

'And you are telling us this mirror truly once belonged to Doctor Dee?'

'The very same,' I said. 'There is a similar object in the collection in the British Museum. But I am not the only one who has always thought it to be a later copy. What you have here is original. I would say the working and jade setting suggest a Pre-Colombian civilisation; though I am no expert, and Professor Chapman – who was – seemed if his papers are anything to go by to prefer a Middle Eastern origin. It was probably seized from Cadiz by Drake. I would guess it was presented to Dee by the Queen herself, as thanks for casting her horoscopes.'

Fisher, for all his initial interest, now seemed curiously disinclined to discuss it. Thinking this was a fallow area in his otherwise comprehensive historical knowledge, and that he might not have appreciated how exciting was the discovery, I decided to ask the table what they knew of Dr Dee.

'I know a little,' said Reverend Simmons, taking up the conversational gauntlet, as Fisher was for once declining the chance to hold forth, 'now let me see. Dee was a great astronomer and mathematician . . . He also advised Elizabeth I on naval matters, and what we would now call the defence of the Realm. Many call him the father of the British Empire – for I believe he first formed the idea – and even coined the phrase. He was supposed to be the cleverest man in Europe. Some thought him mad.'

'He was a magus and a necromancer,' Schwarzgruber interjected rather superciliously, although it is his area, and I confess I always thought myself that Dee was of the Devil's party. 'Do not forget he wrote the Monas Hieroglyphica – the most detailed work on cabalistic cryptology since the Steganographia of Trithemius. It has still not yielded all its secrets to the light of modern scholarship. I am surprised, Herr Reverend, that you are happy to attribute the idea of your Empire to a man who was a magician, a charlatan, a bigamist . . .'

'But science then was in its infancy, Professor-Doctor,' Fisher cut in, rather crossly. 'The boundaries between astronomy and astrology . . . chemistry and alchemy . . . mathematics and numerology – they were not then so clearly defined. Of course there were stories, but those were ignorant times. After all, people said the same of Newton . . .'

'Quite so Warden,' said Simmons, 'for they used to say, I think, that Dee could control the elements. He may have been the model for Shakespeare's 'Prospero', and perhaps for Marlowe's 'Faustus'. They even believed that he had summoned the great wind that destroyed the Armada.'

Fisher gave Simmons a rather fierce glance. Schwarzgruber merely sighed and said:

'You English – always so obsessed with the weather.'

'For myself, I think he was a good man,' said Simmons. 'Though it's true he convinced many that he was not. In any case, Mr James: what is this object?'

'Well it was clearly some sort of votive artefact,' said Fisher, slightly offhand: 'Aztec, perhaps, or Mayan. No doubt used in their religious rites.'

'In that case I worry for Mr James,' said Simmons. 'I would not want to have anything to do with it, if I put any of the credence he does in what he calls the '*malice of inanimate objects*'. What the Aztecs did during their religious ceremonies is a long way from the services in Chapel, gentlemen. And the thought of them would make you beg for the relief of four hymns and one of my sermons; however interminable I make them!'

'It's true the Aztecs knew how to deal with undesirable elements,' Schwarzgruber interjected, with a curious smile. His sense of humour is somewhat Teutonic for my taste. And clearly for Fisher's, too, since he came back – a little hotly I felt – with something like:

'They performed human sacrifice on a monstrous scale. They were awash with the blood of whole Peoples. They would cut the heart from their victims with obsidian knives and show it to them still beating. Then they would eat the flesh. And sometimes wear the skin too, in homage to the deity they called 'the Flayed One'. Perverted offerings to their disgusting Gods. If that is what you mean, Professor-Doctor, I do not care to joke about it.'

'Real '*Lost Hearts*', yes?' said Schwarzgruber, unperturbed. 'Like something from that story of Herr James's, where the old scholar is haunted by the children whose hearts he has removed for the purpose of eating. So amusing . . .'

Simmons came to our rescue by repeating his initial question, which Fisher had, now I think of it, deliberately dodged:

'But what I meant to ask is: it is clearly no ordinary mirror – what is the thing made into?'

I could see that Fisher was for some reason very reluctant to continue. I started to explain myself:

'It is a 'show-stone', Reverend. An aid to divination. Unfortunately we have lost his book of practice, so we don't know exactly what Dee did with it, but he would no doubt have tried to use it for –'

But Schwarzgruber was ahead of me:

'He would have used it for scrying, Herr Reverend.'

"*Scrying*'?' asked Fisher.

'For talking to angels, Herbert,' I said.

'Or to Devils, Herr James.'

'Surely not, Professor-Doctor. "*Angels are bright still –*"

'. . .'*But the Brightest fell*',' cut in Schwarzgruber. 'Is that not what Milton said? The Princes of the air can be creatures of the darkness as well as of the light. I do hope your Doctor Dee knew what he was doing, for certainly he did use a show-stone just like this one. He wrote whole books about the results, in English and Enochian.'

'Enochian? What is that?' asked Simmons. 'It isn't taught at Oxford, is it? Why have I never heard of it?'

'Because it is not a human language,' I answered. 'It was taught to Dee by his scryer, the charlatan Edward Kelley, who claimed he had learned it from the voices he heard in the show-stone. The first voices were heard on the night of March 26th 1583, and then continued on and off for several years. Dee thought it was a seraphaimic tongue, not heard on Earth since the Flood. From what he wrote down it may have something in common with early Hebrew. But it does not obey normal linguistic rules, and is only partly understood.'

Here Schwarzgruber, who had been trying to talk over me in his excitement, finally interrupted:

'They say the voices of the spirits that he summoned with his scrying taught Dee how to control the weather – how to conjure and to disburse storms. They also told him and his apprentice to share their wives in common. Well that did not last long: his wife and all their children died suddenly of the plague. But gentlemen, would an *angel* really counsel such a thing?'

'Ah well, I am not married, Herr Schwarzgruber,' I said. I hardly thought this a suitable subject for discussion, even in jest. Simmons came to the conversational rescue once again:

'We must all be thankful to live in more enlightened times.'

'Hear hear,' said Fisher. 'We can put this Swedenborgian nonsense behind us. Thankfully we have now conquered nature with knowledge, and we live in the light of modern science.'

With that he took his prerogative of having the last word: he called grace and we dispersed.

On the way out of hall Reverend Simmons touched my elbow. Leading me off to the side he lowered his tone and said:

'I was half-serious, you know, about being worried for you. If I had known what you were here for – or that it had to do with Quinbey – I would have said something earlier. Just be careful, won't you? And if anything happens, or you wish to speak to someone, make sure you come and find me right away.'

This curious intervention took me by surprise. I hope the non-committal noises I made in response did not offend him. Though I confess I cannot for the life of me imagine what he meant. Before he could say anything else Fisher had come back to bear me away.

When we were back in his lodgings Fisher started to pace up and down. He was uneasy, and continually looked out of the windows. In all he seems the victim of a bad case of the pips. And they must have communicated themselves to poor Mr Ockham. For when I approached him he fluffed up his tail and went and hid under the sofa.

'I apologise for my familiar,' said Fisher, 'he is usually a deal more friendly, but cats will be cats. Perhaps it is to be expected,' he added, which seemed most odd. I wonder what he meant by that?

It is really rather tiresome: Fisher is displaying all the symptoms of an advanced paranoiac. He spoke at great length and volume about the European situation. At one point he said:

'The Europeans must remember, before it is too late, that they are the trustees of civilization. Yet as we speak – over whole tracts of Europe – the tides of liberty are receding. The great experiment of freedom is only firmly established here – and, I suppose, in America and the Dominions. I must say I fear for it.'

He added that he could discern in history no plot, no rhythm, no predetermined pattern. Only 'one emergency after another, like wave follows wave'. Sometimes in the middle of a personal conversation he gets a far-away look in his eye, a declamatory tone in his voice, and the manner of someone who thinks that he is still addressing the House.

What a terrible thing it would be if he is right about the War. I still can see their faces, all those boys. I cannot bear to think it was for nothing, and that it might all happen again.

Eventually it grew late and I bade him good night. The last thing as he was leaving the study for some reason sticks in my mind. He clasped my hand very tight and looked me in the eye and said:

'Pleasant dreams, Monty – you're a good man, and must have a clean conscience if anyone has.'

Then he half turned on the threshold, and I believe would have said something more. But if so he thought better of it and trudged off to bed.

But now at last I am left alone with the show-stone. Never fully alone, of course – one never is with a mirror in the room. No wonder 'mirror' and 'miraculous' have the same Latin root: *miror, mirari – to view with awe.* And certainly it is difficult not to, when one thinks of who else has looked into it. What great fortune to confirm the find of such an extraordinary piece. If only the Book had also survived. I hope I shall make further progress in my investigations. Perhaps I may even publish something.

Here again is the inscription:

CIADSVOPFELQVIUTCRIEAMACSTORQIVUU
HOQSDAOMSDOIPNITSCRTIIRSHENLMPE!D

A Trithemius cipher? No, no, that won't do. Pythagorean Arithmancy, perhaps, like in the numerological books of Cornelius Agrippa? On balance I think not. Or the Chaldean system proposed by Magnus Albertus? Well, we shall have to wait and see. What a delicious prospect of decipherment to occupy me over Christmas vac! I am somewhat surprised I cannot break it right away. It is presumably of a standard Elizabethan form. And I believe they still refer to me as something of an authority on Dee's own cryptography.

I suppose I could consult Schwarzgruber to see what sense he makes of it, but it would be an embarrassing state of affairs if I needed to ask his assistance. I fear my mind is not what it was. It will insist on wandering. I must stay sharp! But now I am in danger of filling more of my journal with the same old worries and gripes. Enough! I must try as ever to be sanguine. The world is as it should be, or at any rate no worse than it deserves.

In the meantime I feel as happy with the show-stone as any schoolboy on Christmas day. I have set it up with pride of place upon my bedroom mantelpiece. The fireplace itself is large but rather smoky. (And its soot-marks suggest this has been true for centuries.) The rest of the room is dark and just a little draughty. Its coffered oak ceiling and panelling must be part of the original fabric. It occurs to me that these rooms have probably changed little since the days of Warden Woodward, and, in all likelihood, since a very long time before that. That is an odd thought: the man probably slept here in this very bedroom. I go about my invariable superstitious ceremony – just to make certain I am alone – of conducting a search of the room. It is nice to be quite sure of these things. The bed seems extremely comfortable. I shall sleep well here, I think.

2 a.m.

I am not now so sure that I altogether like the thing. The show-stone as I turn it in my hands looks more and more exquisite. But all the same the reflections it gives are really not so pleasant. For a start they are not quite aligned, so that until you angle it right it seems they reflect a subtly different room. And the imperfections (as I suppose they must be) in its surface throw off the most peculiar distortions. Just now, for instance, as I was talking to myself, I thought I caught a sudden dreadful sight behind my back. It made me start and I looked round. And when I brought my gaze back to the show-stone I gasped to see the dark distorted face of my reflection staring out. How ghoulish he looks, that man in the looking-glass world that I know to be me. Half mad, half dead, and tortured with age. I reach up and touch my face, which feels strangely numb. Dark thoughts come into my mind too, of forgotten doubts and shames. Truly I now know *'the rage of Caliban seeing his own face in a glass'*.

A growing feeling of discomfort creeps over me. I am not very good with these things at the best of times. I know full well how I can frighten myself with nonsense. But there is nothing pleasant about fear when it comes in real life. It hardly helps that Mr Ockham, who has somehow got in here through the study, is sat at the window ledge and staring straight out. It is really most vexatious of cats to peer so fixedly where there is nothing at all to be seen. But I almost feel as though the show-stone hums at a pitch just beyond hearing – like the after-echo of the low note on an organ. Perhaps it is reverberating in a draught, and creating some sinister resonance. And of course it seems to watch me as I move around the room. It is a great annoyance. Enough! It is time for bed. I must sleep better than last night, as there is much to do tomorrow. Still, I shall certainly say my prayers.

5 a.m.

Sleep impossible. Intolerable dreams. I have decided to move the show-stone to a less intimate part of the lodgings. A foolish fancy, perhaps, but one that will harm nobody. And I think it will afford me a great deal of reassurance. My sleep from the start was uneasy and oppressed. A dream within a dream.

I was asleep and dreaming, harmlessly enough, that I was back at Kings'; although somehow it was also

Old College. I am talking, of all people, to my sister (goodness knows what she was doing there), and trying, but failing, to light up my pipe. I could not make her see how frustrating this was. That is when she starts to choke. It is a violent and barking suffocation. And eventually I see she is choking on a page of newspaper she has somehow swallowed and is now pulling back up out of her throat.

It is incredible how much paper she had ingurgitated – a full double page spread. It has the crossword puzzle on it. Now she flattens it out on my knees and looks at me expectantly, with a strange and distant smile. She seems not to be herself at all. But the crossword has already been entirely filled in with Enochian: ꞁ ꞁ Ɛ ꞁ ꞁ ꞁ Ꮙ. She then beckons me to the window and points outside.

There are the Old College gardens, covered in snow. On it are visible strange shapeless tracks, though too scuffed up to follow. And then I see that there is, nailed up at the top of the Mound, a scarecrow which seems to be made from my clothes. It appears almost unpleasantly lifelike. Finding myself outside, I climb the steps towards it (though I cannot see it from below). I think my sister is with me but, when I turn to speak to her, I realise I am now alone. Finally I approach the top of the steps, and should be able to see the scarecrow, but I suddenly glimpse instead, though indistinctly, a tall masked figure in black – his arms flung out far to the sides.

Then on the wind I hear a crying scream. I seem to wake up here in bed but in fact am still dreaming. There is the noise again. It sounds like an owl torturing its prey – or a copulating fox – or some such loathsome thing, out there in the cloisters. In my dream I get out of bed and look through the window. It is the same view I see through the window now as I write, although very vivid indeed, and the sky the deepest liquid green.

But that is the least of my worries. Rather what torments me is that weird and awful figure which crawls and drags itself, on stumps, with horrid movements – and unnatural speed – across the cloister lawn. This thing like a man is coming towards *my* window. Just then I hear a sound from the show-stone. I turn around but there is nothing. When I look back out at the cloisters they are deserted. But from the show-stone, as if from great distance, there comes a rasping, lungless laugh. I creep over to it. And though I feel an unspeakable sense of dread I am irresistibly compelled to look into it – and God help me I do. I cannot bring myself to write down what I see.

Then I feel the touch upon my shoulder.

At this point, thank Christ, I woke up. I lay awake for some time trying to think of happier things, as one always does after a nightmare. I even sought (as it were) to distract the baser part of my brain. For it is from there, Aristotle tells us, that dreams emanate. I am soon asleep again and fall into another dream. This time I am back at Eton. It is after Games and I am supervising the showers. There is plenty of hot water and great clouds of steam. I am fortunate for it is the third form. The young boys frolic most amusingly. And then again somehow it is also *that* third form, from when I first taught at the school. God forgive me but I later awoke avec *emissio nocturnalis*. I had thought to be free of that foulness.

My nemesis is not long in coming. In my dream one by one the boys leave to get dressed. But the taps are still running. I go forward and crossly call out to see who is in there. The whole room is now full of steam. I think I see a dreadful canvas face staring back at me. The face has huge black eyes. A cloud of steam obscures it and a noxious foetid smell envelopes me. Then I see it is a young boy at the end of the room. Naked. Hot and pink. He stands quite still and stares at me. He is wearing of all things a respirator: one of those useless flat Phenate masks from the start of the War. I shout at him to take it off. I wish I had not. I had somehow known that that awful laugh I had heard had belonged to him. It was of course young Fanshawe, as I think I knew it would be. But here he is still *pre-pubis*. I pray I may never again see anything like it for *he does take off the mask*. I did not realise what gas did to them.

I am looking again in the show-stone as I sit here writing. I like it less and less. Might it not have brought something in with it? Or called up someone who should not have been woken? A foolish thought, perhaps, yet hardly inconsistent with the rules of folklore. I can't bear to sit in any position where I can't see the room. Even dragging a jersey over my head just now was quite horrid. I somehow got caught in it, and I could not look about me for several seconds. I could not swear it but I almost thought I heard a whisper from the show-stone.

How silly this will all seem in the morning. Too much cheese at dinner, no doubt, and too much of Mr Cockburn's finest. Or the affects of an old wives' tale, a painful memory, and an unfamiliar bed. But Mr Ockham hides under the desk and will not come out. If it were light I might risk lying down. But I dare not sleep, though exhausted to nausea. I will sit up in the study and read Wodehouse until dawn. If only these winter nights were not so long.

December 3rd

Morning

It is good to be up and about after such a disturbed night. Fisher looked at me most curiously over breakfast, but we did not have a chance to speak alone. I think he knows something. I suppose I was rather poor company this morning. The maid was surprised I was staying here alone. She said she had thought both sides of the bed had been slept in, so I must have tossed and turned like anything before I gave up the attempt to sleep. Certainly I am utterly exhausted.

I feel a veil has descended between me and the rest of the World. I have been thinking much about McB, and what we said to one another in room 13 of Preisler's Hotel, and how we hedged ourselves about with reticence. I remember how I stood beside his grave, after the others had gone, and threw in Asphodels from Kings' Fellows' garden. But '*how is it that this lives in thy mind – what seest thou else in the dark backward and abysm of time*?' – the face behind the gate.

No these things are best not thought about.

So after all these years why should I think of them now?

Having taken breakfast I came immediately to Pandemonium to make a proper start on Chapman's papers. I am melancholy enough as I walk through the empty college, and I cannot help wondering where Fanshawe had his rooms. I make my way in thick gloom up the staircase to Chapman's set. I could have sworn I had locked up properly last night. But evidently I did not: here is the door is wide open. There is no sign of disturbance, though – or rather, no sign of *further* disturbance, for even after yesterday's efforts, the papers are in a frightful state. And yet I shall have to go through them all carefully. With these antiquarian pursuits, the Devil is always in the detail.

I fear I shall be here for a couple of days at least, entirely without any company. (Or so I hope, for after last night I wish to avoid a sort of company that might be very undesirable indeed.) The prospect is improved by a low sun, which now bursts its way through fast scudding clouds. I am sitting at Chapman's desk, with my back to the room and the gas fire on high.

I realise there is something wrong with the catch on the door. It has broken off part of the wooden flange which holds it. So, if it is not double-locked, the door swings open from its own weight. I will not sit in this empty building with my back to an open door. But again I cannot quite bring myself to *lock myself in*. Instead I prop it shut with a waste paper basket – soon filling up with the detritus from Chapman's notes. I see now: from what Mrs Fisher said about him 'barricading himself in', I believe he must have had the same system.

But here is another curiosity. His notes contain many pages of writing, most of them practically illegible. They largely consist of attempted translations of words from Enochian. Certain whole phrases he had written down – more or less tentatively – and then crossed out:

'Once open, it cannot be closed';

'What God can save?';

'The place by the three –';

'He/she/it? can see you';

'Fatal words{?}';

and (repeated several times):

'he/she/it is coming'.

Now Chapman had copies of Dee's *Liber Loagaeth* – 'The Book of the Words of God' – and some of his other obscure hermetic writings. But try as I might I could not see which passages he was translating or why. It has been three hundred years since anyone took those books seriously. Any meaning they might have once had is lost. It is commonly accepted that Dee was the victim of either a hoax or of harmless madness.

Of what Chapman was attempting, or why he thought it could be worth what was clearly a great deal of trouble, there was no explanation at all. As time passes I become increasingly tempted by what seems an absurd conclusion: that he has deliberately sabotaged any attempt by another to follow his path. It is highly frustrating: like trying to follow someone through a maze when they are too far ahead of you to see them – and to make matters worse are deliberately covering their tracks. In any case, if there is a path, I seem to have lost it entirely.

Afternoon

Just now I had a nasty shock. Returning after lunch, I had done an hour or two more stumbling about in the labyrinth of Chapman's notes. Suddenly I was jolted round by a loud noise behind me, clearly inside the room. It was the waste paper basket – which I must have stacked carelessly with his papers – falling over under the weight of its contents. This of course relieved the counterweight on the door, which now swung open of its own accord. The few seconds before I realised what must have happened were not so pleasant. I listened for any echo of whatever minute vibration must have tipped the papers over onto the floor. There was nothing. Nothing except that quality of thicker silence that you find in busy buildings when they are empty.

But this too was a little annoying. For I had not been conscious of that silence for hours, but rather if anything its absence. Indeed, now that I thought of it, I had been half-aware of half-noises all day. Nothing you could say was distinctive: occasional creaking and scratching. Only perhaps the sorts of sounds old buildings will make as they breathe and settle.

There had been one exception to this.

It was when I had had my last comfort break. I had descended to the ground floor without discovering a lavatory. There I noticed that – as seems standard in the College – the steps continue down to a basement. This turns out to be an area of toilets and bathrooms. I had had to steel myself to go down there into the dark (for I could not for the life of me find any light switch), but I fear it was something of an emergency. Eventually I discovered a lavatory, and that a very dingy and cold one. As I was going down I could have sworn I heard a footfall above me. I believe it came from the landing I had just left. When I came back up I looked for a light under the doors, to see which of the other rooms was occupied. But there were no lights on in any of them, despite the darkness outside. And settling myself back at my desk I saw something else. The uppermost sheets on which I had been working were not, as by habit I usually leave them, perpendicular to the desk, but carelessly spread at an angle.

It was nothing much, really. Nothing much at all. But odd.

Beyond the Mound, a light in Teddy Hall shows someone there is also working late. Pandemonium is now frightfully cold and echoing and full of strange noises from the pipes. I should be glad to continue my research in the snug warmth of the study in the lodge. But there is simply too much paperwork here to shift. And besides, I hardly want to further disorder his notes, lest I disturb even the vestiges of a system I have not understood. Back to work, Monty: no rest for the wicked. Still, the sooner I can get to the bottom of this, the sooner I can be well away from here.

But there was another unfortunate discovery awaiting me, when I engrossed myself again in Chapman's notes. I had begun to notice recurrences of dark anxieties that seemed to afflict him. I suppose I had spotted some mentions of them yesterday, but thought little of them at the time. The night's entertainment I had enjoyed a few hours earlier now made me sit up and take note. There were marginalia, for instance, that said things like:

'Next to this my own troubles seem insignificant';

'If only I could *sleep*, but that is more or less impossible. The more tired one is the harder it is to sleep, and the more anxious one becomes';

'*Pray God it isn't true!*';

and:

'I am certain I am already watched by one who does not wish the mirror disturbed – and WW saw him too?'

I was making a mental note to ask Fisher who in College had the initials 'WW'. That is when I picked up a volume from a stack by the side of the desk. There was a tall pile of books here I had not yet examined. Opening it at the book-marked page I saw there had been underlined – though by whom I do not know – the single word:

'Incubus'.

Looking at its spine revealed it to be a copy of the Pseudomonarchia Daemonum. The rest of the books in the stack suddenly worried me too. I noticed they were mostly on magic, scrying, and other occult subjects. That is just as I suppose you would expect from one researching an object like this, and reading around an unfamiliar area. What was troubling, though, was the number of powerful grimoires he had managed to collect in one place. There, for example, was a complete copy of the Corpus Hermeticum of Hermes Trismegistus. Here was the Talmud Tractate Middoth, with a commentary by Nachmanides of Amsterdam, here was the Clavicula Salomonis – the Key of Solomon (a very rare copy from Freiburg), and the Codex Gigas (which they used to say was written by the Devil himself), and the mighty Picatrix, and a beautiful edition of the Kyranides in Greek, all the way from Constantinople.

I would have been hard-pressed to amass such a fearsome reading list, even from the libraries of Oxford. Furthermore, these were not books I should have taken much pleasure to collect, for all their rarity and value. Such dark works, so full of sacrilegious immorality, so reeking of the glamour of evil, were hardly the place to begin. A modern commentary, surely, would have given a better grasp of the subject, and a proper historical background and exegesis, with rather less of the disturbing detail. Delving into these works, on the other hand, would be less useful for someone trying to understand the context of Dee's erroneous researches, than for someone attempting to copy them.

I could have told him they would not even give him much help with that. For without Dee's book of practice it would be impossible to know what he was about. No doubt this was evidence of Chapman's uncompromising approach to scholarship, and his contempt for secondary sources.

All the same, though, I felt sudden sympathy for the man and for his new anxieties. They were hardly surprising to one who had immersed himself in such things. What is once read cannot be *un*-read. I believe there are a few books in the great sweep of literature that it is very unwise – indeed dangerous – to open. It seemed that, in his last few days of life, Chapman had read most of them.

He had also of course, as I had, found Warden Woodward's distressing testimony. So why had he left no note of this fact beyond the coded reference I'd followed, despite the excellent proof it gave of how the College acquired the show-stone? It was almost as if he was jealous of the discovery, and did not want to share it. There! – another little shock: 'Woodward' – 'WW'? It seems tonight I had better read some more of that grim text. But what could Chapman have meant?

Finally I found a university diary in one of the drawers of the desk. It was mostly blank. For the 25th November there was an asterisk. There was another on the 28th, which was underlined. On his final day – the 30th – there was the following entry:

'Speak to Simmons re the great question.'

Most disturbingly, perhaps, was the entry for the 1st December, which of course he never lived to see. It read simply:

'Tell Fisher I've had enough.'

That really shook me. I wonder whether Fisher has any inkling of this – of what it meant, or of what it foretold. But of what, exactly, had he had enough? It may not be quite prudent to brood over these topics. I now begin to have misgivings about being drawn into this affair in the first place. But I am determined to go and speak to Reverend Simmons – to try and work out exactly what it was that Chapman feared he had found. If the diary is correct, Simmons must have been the other half of one of the last conversations he had had.

Just now as I was reading this diary I am sure I heard noises from the stairwell, which sounded quite distinctly like footsteps *going down* away from me. I went to the door and opened it a crack to listen. But by the time I had done so the noises subsided, leaving only the impression like the ghost of an echo. Surely I would have known if someone had been up here all the time? Like a fool I strained to listen, and, by the time I thought to look out of the window, it was too late to see whether anyone had come from the staircase. There was no-one visible in the quad, though, and indeed I had seen nobody all day.

It is hardly helps that my hearing is growing so poor. I strain to catch the words of those who speak to me, but I am constantly assailed by background noises. That is no doubt the cause of my recent difficulties in following conversations. In any case, I think my nerves are too drained to do any more work today. I shall go and see if I can find Reverend Simmons, assuming he is around.

Early Evening

The stalls of Old College Chapel, seen in the failing light, were as atmospheric as I had hoped. At first I had not thought Simmons was there. I had walked over to the South semi-transept, to examine the Woodward memorial. I believe that I started to speak to it, saying something like:

'Well, old boy, what did Chapman think you had seen?'

Just then, though, a voice rang out from the crossing behind me. It was Simmons, of course, who had no doubt emerged from a vestry.

'Mr James – can I help you?' he asked. 'I was just locking up.'

'Ah, Reverend,' I answered, 'you gave me a start. I was admiring this rather fine bust.'

He had clearly overheard my mutterings, for he added:

'*Requiescat in pace*. Do you always converse with the dead? I trust that they never answer back?!'

'Actually I was hoping to speak with you. I wondered if I might have a private word. I fear it is rather a delicate matter.'

'I see,' he said, suddenly serious. 'I must say I am not altogether surprised. Well in that case won't you please come and join me at home for a nice cup of tea? My wife will be there, of course, but there is no need for that to trouble us. And I have just finished packing away these 'uncommon' prayer-books.'

'A cup of tea is always welcome. I would be delighted.'

I waited for him to lock up the chapel and then followed him out through the lodge. He lives across the road in Holywell Street in a terrace that belongs to the College. It was a tiny timber-framed cottage, very homely, if rather cramped. In all a more delightful spot could not be imagined. Or rather it would have been delightful, but for one bizarre detail: Simmons' wife. She is now completely paralysed and senile. But Simmons – who must be a saint indeed – nurses her himself (with occasional help from her sister, who was leaving as we arrived). And of course here she was in their drawing room, lolling about in a chair. Simmons showed me into this room and actually introduced her. He bent over her and said, with a sad patient tone:

'This is Mr James, he is a friend.'

Then he disappeared through to a kitchen to make us some tea.

Having been abandoned in this irregular manner I had no idea at all what to do. I foolishly tried some pleasantries. But the poor woman simply stared at me. I was painfully conscious that everything I said could be doubtless overheard from the kitchen. Eventually I panicked. I came out with something grotesque like:

'Oh look! A copy of Higgs on the 'Testament of Solomon'. Intriguing!' – and, grabbing the first book to hand, I sat and pretended to read it.

After an age of tortured silence, Simmons came in with a tea tray and said:

'Nothing personal, Mr James, you see my wife has not spoken to anyone for the last eighteen months. Now, what did you want to talk about?'

I realised at that moment what an extraordinary man he was, and what a tragic life he led, and what an example he set of cheerfulness and Christian charity, in the face of this daily private grief.

We exchanged various pleasantries. Then I took my chance and said I knew Chapman had come to see him, the day before the very night he died. I added that I was looking into some private matters of his, and thought that there might be something rather peculiar going on, of which I wanted to get to the bottom in order to further his work. Whilst I would not, of course, expect the Reverend to breach any confidence, I nonetheless wished to discover anything which might be of assistance, as I sought to complete the poor man's last great academic endeavour.

As I was thus circumlocuting, and tying myself in knots between my curiosity and my good manners, a broad smile was spreading across the Reverend's face. Finally, with a laugh, he held up a hand and said:

'Don't worry, Mr James, I completely understand. There are things about Professor Chapman only myself and the Warden knew. And more, perhaps, that were only known to Chapman, God rest his soul. Of those *psychological* matters that so tormented him at the end . . . I fear I cannot enlighten you. You will doubtless already have heard the stories from any one of the SCR gossips.

'Chapman was a confirmed bachelor, who had had a sort of scandal in his private life. More of a personal tragedy, really, for those who believe in a forgiving God. I would not divulge the facts of it to anyone, even were I in full possession of them, which I am not. Suffice it to say, then, that we are all of us human. And some find it hard to control that part of us which is animal. But even the most unnatural instincts can be conquered, if we know ourselves. And I believe that Chapman had conquered his. At the end these things tormented him and he was worried for his soul; but that after all is surely a promising sign. You see: he came to speak to me of self-destruction. And I feared the conversation was more than academic. But at least he was spared that horrid fate, which is a mercy.'

It was not what I had expected hear. Before I could say anything, he resumed:

'Of his other troubles, though, I think I may allow myself to speak. For they have troubled me also over the last few days. And I would have spoken of them to you before, if I hadn't been worried you would think me a fool. I should be interested to hear your views on them, given your knowledge of . . . such things.'

'Such things?' I asked, surprised,

'Well,' he said, and he frowned, 'for want of a better expression – things that go bump in the night.'

This was a direction of talk that I had half-expected, but certainly took no pleasure from pursuing. Simmons continued:

'I am not sure that I will be able to add much to what the Warden will have already told you.'

Here was news. For Fisher had told me nothing.

'It is clear to us both that poor Chapman was suffering some form of nervous collapse. The result, I am sure, of working too hard – combined with a psychological malaise, or what used to be called a spiritual crisis. It seemed he had become quite concerned about the direction his researches were taking. I remember him asking me several times what I thought of the Testament of Solomon. (That is why I have it out – I see you have found it.) He wanted to know about the modern Christian understanding of the nature of the angelic hosts. We spoke at great length about the heresies of the Gnostics, and the colourful delusions of the Albigensians, Cathars, Templars, and Rosicrucians. Obscure and esoteric stuff. Certainly not the sorts of things that are in the normal remit of the modern Church of England. What exactly he was working on he did not discuss with me. Though I believe it must have been of great interest. He spoke as if others were trying to lay hold of it, and he was anxious about plagiarism. These concerns were weighing greatly on his mind. For, as I believe is often the case, he was afflicted with paranoid delusions, even with visions –'

'Visions?' I repeated, trying to sound off-hand.

'I suppose that is what you would call them,' said the Reverend, frowning. 'You see, he said he thought someone or something was watching him. Who has not had that feeling, at one time or other, above all when beset with anxieties? And of course that put me in mind of John Quinbey, and the old tradition of our college revenant. In fact I told him all about 'the Black Scholar'. Perhaps that supplied his mind with material to project his anxiety. Or perhaps there is something in it after all. Either way, he thought he had seen something, one night in the cloisters last week. Whatever it was had disturbed him. I cannot pretend he was in a good state when I last saw him alive.'

Simmons bent forward to poured out more tea. Then he continued:

'And when I next saw him – *after* he was alive – I shalln't forget that to my dying day. They called me into his rooms to say a prayer. Fisher took it very badly. You see he must have died in a state of considerable distress. He looked as if he had been in such an agony of fear – like a life unwillingly choked off. Of course the facial distortion was simply the muscular action caused by the pain of the heart attack. The two Doctors who examined him both confirmed it is quite common. Indeed I myself have seen the same thing before. We had a similar case back in Spooner's day, when I first took this position. It is not the most pleasant part of my job . . . But you came to tell me of your concerns, Mr James, not to listen to mine.'

'So you knew Spooner?' I asked.

'Oh yes,' he said. 'And yes, he really did speak like that, when he was excited. 'The Lord is a shoving leopard', 'God Save the queer old Dean', and so on. He used to get so cross with himself when it happened, but it always had us in stitches.'

'Tell me more, Reverend, of the figure in black.'

Simmons gave me a cautious look, as if to test whether I was in earnest. Seeing I was he lent forward and spoke in a lower, more urgent register:

'*Well!* I have never encountered anything myself. But Jenkins is the man to talk to about this – he says he has seen it in the flesh. Do I believe him? I do not think it is impossible. The Bible tells us that the spirit can survive the body's death,' here he paused, and I was once again conscious of the silent presence of his wife, 'I see no absolute reason to think they may not sometimes be seen by the living. Although, unlike Chapman, I do not believe they can harm us. As for the 'Black Scholar', the best thing would be to speak to Jenkins.'

'When does he come on duty?' I asked, 'I have an interest in this sort of thing, and would be pleased if you introduced me.'

'Certainly. He may be on now – let us go and see him together. He is always good value, at any rate.'

All this while, I hope, I managed to hide from Simmons the effect his words were having. The more I learn the less I like it.

We finished our tea. Simmons went and fussed his wife a little, and told her he would be back in a few minutes. It is a habit, I suppose, for she showed no sign at all of comprehension. It was a great relief to be away from that room, with its awful living inhumation, and back out in to the world of Life. The breath in one's lungs tasted sweet and heady, as it does when one has sat in a room with Death, or Life that might as well be Death. I breathed it deep as we walked back across the road towards the Porters' lodge.

But it turned out Jenkins was not on duty that night.

Instead it was his younger colleague Martin, who was somewhat put out by our visit:

"*Knock knock! – In the other Devil's name!*" said Simmons, startling him from a doze with a Shakespearean broadside, 'Look lively, Man – '*Remember the Porter!*'"

'Oh Sir! – I'm sorry: I didn't see you there.'

Simmons introduced me, and asked him if he had seen anything suspicious round the Bell Tower the previous week.

'Not me, Sir, begging your pardon,' he said, 'I wasn't even on duty last week. That would have been Old Jenkins. But he wouldn't have gone in there either, I reckon.'

'And why not?' said Simmons.

'He won't even go into the cloisters after dark,' said Martin with a chuckle, before hurriedly adding. 'Or rather he goes in at the entrance, of course, and shines his torch round, and says: 'is there anyone there – no? Oh good!' and then he's straight off out of it. But he won't go round the Bell Tower side, nor stay any longer than he has to. He saw something there once, see, and it right gave him the willies it did. If you'll, err, pardon the expression, Sir.'

'What did he see?'

'Well, I ain't saying as *I* believe it. But Jenkins's a good man, you know, and one of the best Porters in Oxford. Well, the way *he* tells it, and you'd be better off hearing it from him, mind, but the way he tells it it's like this: he's doing his rounds early Boxing Day morning – there's no-one else in the College then, see, and it's quiet as you like. It's very late and he'd have been very tired I expect' [and hardly sober either, I thought, on that night and knowing what they said of him] 'he's just checking the old Gate, and coming back into Great Quad, when he passes someone heading to the cloisters. He says 'Good Night' to him

81

but there's no reply. 'Bloody rude', he thinks – that's his words Sir – 'bloody rude'. And then he remembers that there's no-one left in college over Christmas, nor any good reason they'd be heading towards Chapel or the Cloisters, not at that time of night least of all. Well, of course, when he turns round the figure's gone.'

'What did he look like, this . . . *figure*?'

'He was wearing a strange long cloak, like a gown, but going all the way round like. As for his face, well, he won't tell me that . . . but he didn't like it one bit!'

'What did he do?'

'Do? Well, he was scared, which is – well – it's unlike him. So at first he stays in Great Quad to see if anyone comes out. That's the only way in or out of the Cloisters, you see. But no-one comes. He just stands there, he says, in the open. Waiting. Then after twenty minutes or so he thinks he'd better pull his finger out of it. He takes a deep breath and goes to have a look. He went through and checked Chapel and there's nothing up there, so out he goes into the Cloisters. Goes all round them he does, and there's nobody there. But that's strange too though, 'cause there's no other way out this fella could've gone. Jenkins stands in the middle of the Cloisters, looking back at Chapel, and it's as quiet as the grave . . . and then suddenly: WALLOP!' Martin thumped his desk with a sudden startling crash, which made Simmons jump, 'A small branch only come off the tree and dropped in the leaves behind him. Ha! At that (he tells this better than me, Sir), at that he screams 'oh b—' – well, you can guess what he screams – and he runs for it. Doesn't stop til he gets back here!'

Martin had clearly heard this story many times, but he still laughed at that. Then he sighed and continued:

'Of course that's not the first time. People have always

said those Cloisters are a bad place – that there's some-thing wrong with 'em. I don't like 'em myself, I can tell you that, when it's late and out of term. A quick look in and that's enough for me, thank you very much.'

'But have you ever had any . . . unwelcome encounters, around the College after dark?' said Simmons.

'Me Sir?' asked Martin, suspiciously. 'No of course not – I don't believe a word of it. It's just folks scaring themselves over nothing. I'm no fool. What do you take me for?'

'Thank you Martin,' said the Reverend, somewhat deflated, 'that'll be all.'

'Goodnight, Sir. Sir. Er – welcome to College.'

We walked back into the College, until we stood out of Martin's earshot.

'Well,' I said, 'I don't see that persuading the Sad-ducees. It seems that everyone's heard Jenkins tell that story. Chapman would have known it too. And so by the way would anyone who wanted to commit a theft and not be interfered with.'

'You think there's someone in College up to no good?' asked Simmons, shocked. 'That, I simply cannot bring myself to believe.'

'That's what the Warden thinks,' I said. 'But who or why is a total mystery to me.'

With that Simmons wished me goodnight, leaving me in little better spirits than he had found me. The tradi-tion of the 'Black Scholar' was an interesting one. The more so if it had grown from a genuine folk-memory of real events of the deep past. I walked quickly back to the Warden's lodge. Whatever Chapman thought he had seen, the answers might be found in my old friend Woodward:

Part 4 – The Enormous Machinery of Hell

'The first Plague that fell unto Man,
was the want of Science.'
　　　　　　Spoken by 'Aath' to Dee, in Chrystallo

'It was a Milliner's wife call'd Sarah Jeffreys, who dwell'd over at St Clement's by the Meadow, who first brought that Evil into Oxford. Coming across old Magdalen Bridge one Morning with a Parcel of Hats, she stagger'd, and then fell down in the Dirt with a Scream, and those that ran to help her found she had the fearful Signs upon her neck, so that they stood off from her again, and would not come close to her, indeed she lay there for some time uttering horrible Cries, and had Blood Vomiting. And still none would help her, til they sent someone to find her Husband, who at last came and took her Home, berating them that found her as being most un-Christian. He was frighten'd of her also, though, and was right to be so, as she was at the very Pinch of Death, so that he could do nothing for her, and she was dead within the Hour, and he the next Day, and all their four Children with them.

They were limed and buried at Night. But the Physick who attend'd them put it out that it was no Plague that had carried them off, but rather the Sweating Sickenesse, though all knew what it really was, and yet the Magistrates still did nothing, but said the Town remain'd free of the Pestilence, though in Truth all knew the Sweates were as infectious and productive of Mortalitie as the Plague. And yet the foolish Townsfolk still went about congratulating themselves on their good Fortune, and would not hear of any Talk that the Plague was come into Oxford, and did rail at anyone who said it, as if the Citie were confront'd with a monstrous Devile, face to face, and yet for Feare would never look it in the Eye.

Indeed for ten Days after there were no other Cases, and it seem'd with God's Grace that we might yet be spared. But then in the third Week after Michaelmas, on the very same Day, there were two more Outbreaks of the Distemper: a Family in St Clement's and a Butcher here in the Towne. Now at last the Citie did awake, though it was as from a Dream into a Nightmare, and the Magistrates did shut up the Houses and declare a Curfew, but it was too late, for the Sickenesse was upon us, and spread violently, and was got into our Parish the Week following. Now at last there were great Feares of it through the Citie, it being said that two dozen more Houses were shut up, and that the Towne grew very sickly, and all the People were now afear'd of it. But yet they did not know the first of it, for the Authorities, as if jealous of the Knowledge that they had, and fearful of losing the Power and Trust they wield'd, direct'd the greater Part of their Effort into giving false Report, to reassuring the Populace and preventing Panick, rather than to combating the Distemper.

Though in Truth there was little enough that could by then be done, for the Disease despised all Physick. The Chirurgeons and Empirics sold diverse sovereign Poultices and Cordials, but none could stop those fatal Sores, Swellings, Tumours, and Carbuncles, that did run and break and decompose the Skin, or the Apoplexies and

Delirium and Blood Vomiting, so that almost all who caught it, died fearfully within Days or Hours in utmost Pain.

A Decree went out that all the Cats and Dogs and diverse Livestock in the Citie should be kill'd, being unwholesome Creatures, and dumb Beasts incapable of Government. But no Provision was made for their removal, so that their Bodies were everywhere in the Towne by the Way, or in Ditches, where they began to bloat and stink. Clouds of great fat Flies did swarm upon them as they fester'd, and did then fly off, spreading perhaps the Infection with them as they flew. It was noticed, and indeed I saw with my own Eyes, that the Rats which did feed upon these putrid Carcasses, and were great gorged things of prodigious size, themselves grew sicke and died, so that there were everywhere too the Corpses of Rats. And yet the Night-soil men, or those that had not yet the Distemper – for some of their Number were amongst the first to die – grew afear'd of their Profession, and would not come out, so that there was throughout Oxford a general welling up of Filth.

I myself resolved to go out into it no more, except when it could not be help'd, and began to take a double Dose of the bitter Mercurial Panacea – though it made me sick to the Bowels – and to say my Prayers no longer three but rather six Times every Day. Certainly the Citie has no good Ayre: the poisonous Vapours arising from the Earth, and the Dampness from the Rivers and the Marshes, co-mingle with the stagnating Ayre within the Narrow Lanes, and grow into a Pestiferous Miasma, that hangs above the Towne in a great infectious Stench.

As for the University, the other Heads of Houses all almost to a one, and many of the Fellows too, now fled to the Countrie, where they depend'd on safety, some Colleges having houses set aside there for a Refuge, though it seem'd but doubtful, the whole of England being now afflict'd, whether 'twas safer to go or stay. Our College having no such Refuge, and all those that could leave having already depart'd, I instead resolved to stay: to close the College up, safe behind our stout Walls, that none would come in or out. And to keep Fires burning Day and Night in the Quadrangle against those Fumes, Sweats, Stenches, Breaths, and Exhalations of the Sick – which I suppose, by attacking sound Persons in their Vital Parts, may bring the Sickenesse on us, so that every Breath we take is a Wager for our very Lives – and in this way we might ride out the monstrous Storm that was come upon Oxford.

To that End I instruct'd the Manciple to gather as much salt'd fish and cured Ham and Victuals as could be had, from the Merchants in the Streets of Towne that were not yet stricken, together with Barrels of small Beer, and some of those excellent fruit Pies they sell in Turl Lane (for it would be no goode Thing to starve ourselves this Plaguetime), and, with the Vegetables grown in our own Gardens, it seem'd more than likely we could ride out the Storme of Death that raged about us. There were, besides, hopes of a great Frost that would freeze out the Infection, though our stubborn Winter remain'd unnaturally warm and wet, as if the Elements themselves conspired to make us ill.

Throughout this time I knew that upon my Shoulders fell the entire Dutie to save the College, to protect its Members both in their Bodies and their Souls, and in Truth it was a heavy Burden. They all look'd to me for Decision and for Succour. I have found it hard enough to get either Peace or Sleep throughout these dreadful Weeks, so that my Heart has been sore worn out, and my Face, reflect'd in the Looking-Glasse, looks at me like my Father used to do, when he was an old Man beaten down with Care.

I stay'd as much as I could in College, though I did go abroad one Evening before Curfew and happen'd – by pure Chance – to walk through Magpie Lane, that they did lately call Gropecunte Lane, as used ofttimes to be my wont, and was curious to watch and see if they continued there their Cyprian trade, even in this Plague-time.

Indeed there was one comely Wench, by that part of the lane by the Magpie Inn, that I recognised as daughter of William the Butcher. I spoke to her, 'tis true, and said kind Words to her, but I swear I did never touch her filthy Bodie (nor have I ever yet polluted myself in that way since my Resolution).

I told her that the Infection was growing to its chief Violence, and that it was spread by Touch, and that Death sometimes came without Warning of Symptoms, so that she might not even know who carried the Distemper. Furthermore, the Mayor had decreed, that the Infect'd were to be permitt'd the Libertie to go abroad at Night, when Darkenesse fell, to fetch Food from the Lazar-house that was left there to them, or to slake their awful Thirsts, so that soon it would be not safe. She said that her Father was sicke and they had no Monie for Food. I left her some copper Pennies on the Ground – for it was unclean to touch her – and told her to go Home, and I did nothing wanton with her, comely as she was, so that I believe I commit'd then no Sin, nor did I offend God's Will.

I had hoped that Quinbey would chuse to go from hence, that the College might be the safer without the Impurity of his Presence. But as the Day appoint'd for the closing up approach'd he show'd no Sign of making Preparations to depart. Indeed he seem'd quite unconcern'd with the Disaster that was come upon us, and his want of Feare did trouble me. To this end, even amongst the Preparations, I resolved to visit him in his Chambers the day before the College was to be shut up, to tell him that it might be better for him to take himself away from hence, whilst he had yet the Chance.

I knock'd on the outer Door of his Rooms (for he would never sport his Oak). He open'd it a Crack and look'd out with one wild Eye.

'Ah Warden,' he says, 'I feare I am frightful busy.'

'But what exactly are you busy with, Sir?' say I.

He seem'd reluctant to open the door, and indeed there were Papers and Apparatus so strewn across his Floor that this were no easy Task. A musty Smell was in there, too, and I breath'd through a Napkin. I push'd past him to his Desk, on which, betwixt great Piles of Papers, I saw Star Charts, Astrolabes, Celestial Globes, Vials of Quicksilver, and glass Vessels in which were floating nameless Horrors, Prodigies, and the Changeling Tithes of Lilith (including one that had been born – and for an Hour lived – and suck'd! – but had no Head above the Mouth, and no true Brain, and was but an amorphous Mass of shuffled human Organs, Bones, Bowels, Viscera, and other monstrous Parts). On his Papers there were diverse weird Symbols too, that I look'd at but could make no sense of, and Writing that I could not read. Fearing now the worst, I demand'd to know what in Heaven's name he had been working on so feverish and late into the small Hours of the night.

'I have turn'd away from Paracelsus', he said, in haughty Tones. 'I follow now my own Direction. Even you will know of the Rainbow that Men see in a Piece of

Glass. But did you know the same can be seen with my own Eyes if I do this!'

And with that he grabb'd a bronze Nail or Bodkin, and wrapp'd it with thin Leather, and work'd it betwixt his Eye and the Socket, and behind the Eye, which was thus distort'd and stared out at me most fearfully, and he cried out with Pain and Triumph that he saw it.

'And if,' he said, 'you take the Eye of a Person newly dead, and you cut away the Membranes at the Back to expose the Humour, without spilling any, and then put this Eye in the Hole of a Shutter, so that its Front faces diverse Objects lit up by a Candle. If you then look through it you will see there a Picture of all those Objects – and if you squeeze the Eye just a little the Picture is distort'd, and you may see a Rainbow.

'Images are form'd in this way at the back of the Eye and pass from thence into the Mind, so our Soul – if Soul we have – gains Knowledge of the World. Yet we must have a care to distinguish those Qualities, such as Number, Shape, and Size, which do really have Existence in the World. These are quite unlike those Secondary Qualities, for instance Colour, Taste, and Smell, that have no true Existence beyond the corpuscular or minute Parts which have the Power to produce Sensation, Pain, or Sickenesse in us, and are created rather by our Mind. For the Things that appear to our Senses, along with Beauty, Goodness, and Feare, lie indeed in the Eye of the Beholder, and must be kept in Doubt.'

At that he shew'd me, with a Flourish, on a Clerk's Table in the Corner, a fearful Instrument of Brass, in which was held with clamps: a real Eye.

'My God!' I cried, 'Then you have look'd through dead Men's Eyes.'

He said nothing to deny it.

'I wonder – what have you seen?'

At this he laugh'd and said:

'A thousand Colours, Warden; a thousand beautiful Things.'

'Such Knowledge is Diabolical!'

'No. All Knowledge is Power. We must un-learn our Feare at looking.' He beckon'd me to a large brass Object on his Bench.

'What is that?' I ask'd him.

'A type of Microscopia', he said. 'It is the Inverse of a Telescope, such as the other Virtuosi in the Invisible College use for watching the Heavens. There are hidden Worlds all around us, Warden, that no-one heretofore guess'd at, and are not mention'd in the Scriptures, and invisible Creatures too, that are on us and in us. With this Device we can see them. I would understand these hidden Worlds, and how the World we see insinuates itself into the Eye, and how the Mind controls what we see. I have direct'd my internal Meditations to destroy all false Opinion. But I am still beset by that Malicious Demon, who makes me believe that what I see and think are real, when they are but base and empty Lies, that will bring us to believe in Anything.'

'Tell me, Sir, is that worse than believing in Nothing? These 'internal Meditations' of which you speak are foolish Nonsense.'

'But Warden, Doubt is what has brought us thus much higher than the Savages. We must doubt Everything.'

'Even God?'

He would not answer that, but just stared at me, and he smiled strangely, as one who is Brainsick. With that I grew frighten'd, and cried:

'Heavens, Man, there are no Hidden Worlds!'

'In that case you will look in the Device?'

'I am not afraid,' I said, and I look'd into it. I saw at first Nothing, but then, dimly glimpsed in the Candle-light, I did suddenly see strange and fearful Shapes, that seem'd like Creatures, or rather like Dragons, Serpents, and Deviles, monstrous to behold. Now I cried out:

'What new and horrid World is this? 'Hell is empty, and all the Devils are here!' What do you show me? Do I look through another's Eye?'

'Not through, but at!' he laughed. 'It is the aqueous Humour of the Eye of a Man,' {no doubt, I now realise, one lately dead of the Distemper}, 'What you see are the tiny Creatures, or Animal Spirits, that did dwell inside the Eye.'

'I will not believe it!'

'Then believe this: here is a Flea, seen as it really is!'

I look'd again and there I saw a monstrous Thing indeed, for here was a Beast, without doubt the same shape as one would say of a Flea, but many times enlarg'd, and construct'd from many perfect tiny Parts, which seem'd to show indeed the Truth of what he had said. In that hor-rid Moment perhaps he cast some Spell on me, for there came into my Mind a blasphemous Idea, and with it came Despair. Yet I answer'd him thus:

'I know not what you shew me, but I know that God is real. He loves and would not deceive us. As for the Soul – that better part of us that will survive the Corruption of our Bodies – that you dare doubt that it exists shows only that yours is in the direst Need of saving. It is just as I fear'd when we found you were meddling with that necromantic Looking-Glasse.'

At this he laugh'd to my Face, but I point'd at the sever'd Eye and continued: 'And besides, Sir, by what

Authoritie do you conduct these Devilish 'Experiments', against the Law and all good Christian Custom? When I was young we knew what to call Men like you, and how to deal with you. And at a time like this-'

'A Time like what, Warden?'

'Fear you not, Man? The Plague is Come!'

'And yet 'God loves us'!'

''Great Plagues remain for the ungodly: but whoso putteth his trust in the Lord, Mercy embraceth him on every Side'. This is the Devile's Work, and little Wonder there is Plague, when the Times see such Blasphemies as this.'

'Oh but there have been Plagues before, Warden', he said. 'The Great Mortalities of the Third King Edward. The Plague of Justinian, which came up out of Egypt. The great Distemper that, says Galen, kill'd the Emperor Antoninus, and one in three of his Romans. The Plague of Hippocrates in Athens, from which the Greek Historian tells us that no Feare of God nor Law of Man did give restraint; and as for the Gods, it seem'd to be the same thing whether one worshipp'd them or not, for the Good and the Bad died entirely indiscrimate. So what should this Visitation signify, when the People flock to the Churches and do there infect each another? What has this to do with God?'

'Are you then a Hobbist?' I answer'd. 'And what if you were right? Your Unnatural Philosophy starts with Dabblings in the disputed Borders of Nature, but mark me ends with dethroning God Himself, and your 'Malicious Demon' would be Emperor of the Earth; or else Nobodie would be. The whole World would be no more than a meaningless Swamp of Lust and Cruelty, and the Commonwealth of Man, without Moralitie or Government, would fall into the Diabolick Conflict of Each against Each.'

'I see it! In the Battle between Truth and Illusion you are for Illusion!'

'In the War betwixt Good and Evile I am for Good!'

'Truth and Goodenesse may not be Allies but grievous Enemies. Nature is no Friende to us: she is our bitter Foe, or rather she cares not for us at all, whether she destroys us or no. We cannot yet alter this, though we can set our Minds to it as Men.'

'We can do much more than that, Sir,' said I. 'For I intend to keep the Pestilence out of this College. If you will not be gone then confine yourself to your Chambers.'

At this he became suddenly anxious, and ask'd if his Sister could enter to stay here for the Duration. That was a way of his – he seem'd not to understand, for all his Learning, the Sentiments his actions produced in others, nor thought it Strange, to insult with one Breath and seek Favour with the Next. I said it could by no means be allow'd, it being against the Statutes of the College, and all Propriety. At this he grew violently enraged, and utter'd most irreligious Oaths and Curses, and call'd me Tyrant, Hypocrite, Whoremonger, Knave, and Roast-Beef Puritan, and grabb'd his Stick – with which he would have struck me. At this I ran out, for in his Rage I was sore afraid of him.

Next day I made the final Preparations for the shutting up, which was urgent indeed, given the Mortalitie by then in the Towne. But I did it no longer with Pleasure, but rather Foreboding, to be lock'd up with such a Man, as a Demon in our very Midst.

Whether indeed we had lock'd the Evil out, or rather lock'd ourselves in with it, the Day of the shutting up came none too soon. For on the last Day before we closed and barr'd the Gate, I went forth myself one last Time on diverse Errands, and to tell the Magistrates and the Mayor what it was that we intend'd. The condition of the Citie was now indeed grown most fearful. She was like a wound'd Animal, that in Pain and Feare cries out and knows itself no longer, nor can by any means be govern'd.

Going out through the Lodge into College Lane, with a Pomander about my Neck, the sweet and sickly Stink of the Towne immediately overcame me, and there was indeed in that no doubting the Evidence of my Senses. The Perfume, I suppose, of Putrefaction, and of suppurated and ruptured Buboes, mix'd into a deadly Effluvium that hung throughout the Towne. I resolved to breathe, as much as it were possible, through a sprig of Rosemary that I did now hold up to my Face.

The Day was warm and wet, and my new Collar chafed upon my Neck. I touch'd the outside of my right Hand, as was my wont, along the rough Stonework of the Wall of the Lane – which is the outer Wall of the Cloisters – but it came to my Mind that I must on no Account touch any Thing outside the College, lest it, the Earth, and the very Stones themselves be impregnated with those poisonous Insects, or rather minute Animals, or their Eggs, which as it seems float hidden all about us in the noxious Ayre. I put on my Gloves, but I could still feel and was most unpleasantly aware of that part of my Hand, which had touch'd the Wall, and the sensation stay'd with me, and I resolved to scour and wash it in Vinegar, as soon as I return'd, which indeed I later did.

I had fear'd it would be hard enough to move through the Streets, without touching the filthy Bodies of the People in the Crowd, as they might brush past me. There were but few abroad, though, and those there were kept their Distance. I look'd carefully about myself but could see Nobodie with the Distemper, thank God, nor had I any wish to. But there were Houses, even in Holy Well Street hard up against the College, that were shut up, with the fearful red Cross upon their Doors. I took care to stay to the Middle of the Streets, which were in any case full of Mud and Filthe, and to touch nothing, and, when I arrived at the Guildhall, to knock at and push with my Feet the Doors through which I walk'd. The suffocating Ayre in that part of the Citie was as bad as any I've breath'd.

I sought out the Mayor, to inform him that we were to shut up the College, which I expect'd him to oppose, though he had not the Prerogative to do so. When I enter'd the Room in which he was, he bade me sit, but I said I would not, for it suddenly came into my Mind that I knew not who else had sat down there, and whether or not they were Infect'd.

The Mayor himself seem'd to have despair'd:

'Do as you will. My Authoritie here is at an end.'

'What are you saying, Man? You are the Government in this City! Who will keep the Peace?'

'The Peace – ha!' says he, full of Sorrow. 'What else can be done? The Time is most calamitous. There is not any College nor Hall but yours which has not lost some to the Infection, so that within the past twelve Days have died two hundred Scholars, and Citizens without Number. The Pest-House is full. The Physicks are all dead. The Graveyards and the Pits do over-flow. The Dead lie rancid in their Houses where they fall. We run out of Men who will bury them. What did we do, Master, that God has call'd this Horror down upon us?'

I stopp'd myself from speaking as I would about the Government of the Kingdome, and of this Citie, and merely repeat'd the Words of the Good Book:

"And the Lord sayeth: there will be Blood throughout all the Land of Egypt, both in Vessels of Stone, and in Vessels of Wood."

'Well Master, you are a learned Man. But for my Part I will not believe this is God's Punishment. Most of the Clergy – or rather those that did not flee – have fallen with the Sickenesse. It makes no exception for the Good or the Devout, nor discrimination betwixt the worst Rakes and the most pious Men, whether High-Church or Dissenters.

'Indeed, those who from Kindenesse or Bravery go to help others have bourn the heaviest Toll. Reverend Theakston, who bravely went to minister to the Dying, and made the others ashamed that would not also, died raving with Agonies in his own Filth by Cornmarket, and the Beaters had to take him to the Pit. Yet I know of several Villains, who have not the Sickenesse, and one Rogue in the Prison who is said to have recover'd.

'The Innocent it seems are never spared. Brothers, Sisters, Parents, Children, Friends – all carry Death home with them to the ones they love and do thus Destroy their entire Families with their poisonous Embraces. Two days ago the Watchmen were call'd by Neighbours, who were offend'd by the Stench, into a House that had not been shut up, in St Giles, from which moreover they had heard an Infant crying. They found that all in the House were Dead, and some so liquefied and rott'd away, that it was with Difficulty they were carry'd, so that picking up each End, the Middle would fall through, and yet there lived a Baby, that did suck upon the Breast of its Mother, who was long-since dead of the Plague, and the Child itself alive yet, but infect'd.

'What can be said in the Face of such Evile? What more can be done? And all the while its Fury still increases: nobodie knew it could run with so much Rage and Violence. Another such a Month as this and there will be none of us left with Eyes to weep.'

After that he told of Folk driven to Madness by the Violence of the Pain of their Swellings, that do run through the Streets raving, and do hurl themselves deliriously headlong into the River – so that there are bloat'd Bodies floating on the Water, that have to be fetch'd out with long Poles and Hooks – and some leap wailing into Wells, which pollutes the Water, or into the very Pits where, for want of those to bury or to mourn, or Space on hallow'd Earth, the Multitudes of the Dead are simply thrown in Heaps, and Nobodie dares go in to fetch them out, so that there are some *limed and buried even who were not yet dead.* After that he told another Storie, of a young Girl from Woodstock, so dismal and so grievous, and told with such an horrid Way of talking, that I shall draw over it a black Cloth of Silence, for even now I cannot bring myself to utter it.

'If this is not God's doing, sent to punish us,' I ask'd, 'then what say you is the Cause of these Disasters?'

At this he lower'd his Voice, as if confiding in me:

'Some say the Infection is spread by Luciferians and Papists, who do use Dark Magick and Poison in their Designs. Strange Persons have been seen abroad at Night, and there are many Foreigne Folk come into the Town. You would not credit how many cases we have had of Murther, or Actions as good as Murther. Oh Mankind, look at your Reflection! – what Horrors lie within you?

'For many of the Infect'd fall into a dreadful Frenzy of Hatred, and do willingly attempt to blight their Neighbours, so that we must lock them up or tie them down til they themselves be dead. Whether it be the Distemper itself, or rather a Fury against their own Kind, as if there were a Corruption, not only as a Symptom of the Plague, but Latent in the very Soul of man – an Evile such that we cannot bear to see Ourselves more wretched than each Other, and would do anything to make all Others as miserable as Ourselves.'

'But what Christian would act in so monstrous a Fashion?'

'Only one for sure under the Power of Witchcraft!' he whisper'd. 'This evile Madness spreads as fast as the Infection, so that People become wilde with Feare and would do any Thing, to save themselves or be revenged on Others. The Forces of Darkenesse surely lie behind it. Remember Signore Mora, who they burn'd in Milan for Plague-spreading. We have many Reports of Others of his like amongst us now. We must employ the same Vigilance here. If we only had a Witchfinder or a Matthew Hopkins, we should soon put the Fear of God in them. How would you explain it else? Witchcraft is in Oxford, of that I have no Doubt!'

I saw then that the Mayor was given up to Hysteria and sick Fancies, and I wasted no more Words saying that he should look to God, and not to invent'd Deviles. I took my Leave, being careful as before to touch Nothing and no Bodie. As I return'd I could see a great Bonfire outside the Bodley Schools, for they were burning all the Books which had in them any taint of Dissent, or Levelling, or Papism, or the 'New Learning', or Alchemical and Necromantic Texts. Oxford had surrender'd to an Epidemic of Feare, and was fright'd to Death with the Terror of these Times, and I saw that Feare itself can destroy a Citie. For Neighbours do lie and inform against each Other, that Others might be shut up and not themselves. Husbands and Wives turn against each other in Feare, and they are fearful of even their own Children. Men that had been Friends infect each other – either through Malice or through their careless Terror. Even its Government is so awed for Feare that it breaks down, so that all Order, Religion, Law, Moralitie, and Peace are lost, and Everywhere a Commonwealth of Darknesse reigns.

They say that to support the Spirits and avoid the Feare of it is the best Preventative of the Pestilence. Which were easy enough to say. But for myself I found my cowardly Heart to discover a monstrous Feare in me. As I was returning, on the Corner of Broad Street, a young Boy of a sudden ran out and grab'd my Arm, and beg'd for Monie for Food, saying that his Parents were dead of the Distemper, and he had Nothing to eat. God forgive me! – I cried out and knock'd him down, for I would not have him touch me, and he scream'd at me and ran off, though Truth be told I was as afraid of him, as he of me, and by God this Plague has made me as cruel as any Beast.

At this I hurried back to College, and had them bar the Gate, and let None in or out for any Reason, so that we were now alone on our own Devices, for better or for worse, and we would live or die together.

When I had done this I felt my Feare leave me, but then I thought of the Mayor's Words, and of the terrible Curse of Witchcraft. Could it be true? The ignorant common People, when any Catastrophie befalls them, always seek to lay the Blame upon a human Agency, needing as they do some *Person* to reproach for their Miserie. They are happy in their Feare to dream up Dark Forces to condemn, at the very Time they give themselves up to vain un-Christian Superstitions. For just as the same Folk rail against Witchcraft, they adopt any Number of foolish Preventatives. Physicks and Quack-Doctors give diverse medical Accounts and Panaceas, but they too are carried away, indeed faster than the Rest. Some say, I hear, that you must not mention the Name of any one who has died. Others that a Doll, or Figure of a Green Man, worn about the Neck, will ward off the Evil Eye, and with it the Distemper. Others still that certain Words, writ on Bread and swallow'd, will protect him that eats them, as if the Words themselves had Power. And at the same Time they seem to feare Black Magick, as much or more than the Disease itself, which kills them!

Yet in Truth so much Suffering and Pain could hardly be without Reason. And it can surely not be Natural – a mere random deadly Exhalation from the Earth. Was it then the Breath of the Almighty that blew across our Citie?

But then I thought again of Quinbey's Doings, and of his 'Invisible College', and of the strange Companie he had been seen to keep (no doubt of Scryers and Planetarians), and of his previous dealings with the Mirror, and then indeed the Matter seem'd less certain. In his Experiments it is clear there was Alchemie at least, from whence 'tis but a single Step to the attempt of Witchcraft. And then it seem'd most strange, that our College alone was not afflict'd, which I had previously put down to my own Care, but now I wonder'd whether there might not be another Explanation.

I resolved to increase my Knowledge of such Matters, and began to make a Study of the Formicarius, the

Malleus Maleficarum – the famous 'Hammer of the Witches', the Tractatus De Praestigiis Daemonum, the 'Demonolatry' of Remigius, the Daemonologie of King James, and the Fustis and Flagellum Daemonum of Hieronymous Menghi, which learned Christian Authors all do give Weight to the Observation that Witch-craft is a real and common Evil in Mankind, albeit more common to Women than to Men, because of the inherent Wickedness of their Hearts. There were many Cases report'd too, from many Countries, of Witches spreading Poisons and Disease.

I also render'd into English the rest of those Parts of the *Liber Sextus* that were writ in the Celestial or Adamical Language (for which Purpose I had resort to the Claves Angelicae – the Angelic Keys – by that same learned Author). Here was a monstrous Thing discover'd! For whether in Mistake or Malice or Despair, the Writer describes in that ante-diluvian Tongue what evil Thing must be done, by any who wish to use the Mirror, without placing themselves thereby in direst Danger. If Quinbey had done such a Thing, then his Soul would be damn'd indeed, and 'twas as well I took it off him when I did. Though, again, I had no Proof that he had done it.

I decided in any event that Quinbey should be made safe, without alerting the other Fellows, who would doubtless support him. Accordingly I mount'd to the Top of his Stair (his Chambers being set apart on the uppermost Floor) and knock'd thrice upon his outer Door.

I heard a great Commotion inside, as though he were concealing some of his Papers. He open'd the Door directly, and he would in no ways let me enter (though I could see the Room over his Shoulder but could see not what he had conceal'd). I told him that, as there had been some Complaints against him, and for his own Good, he must either leave the College, or, if he would not, he must submit to be lock'd up in his Chambers, with a Watch set on his Door, and Food would be deliver'd to him whenever he wish'd.

I had expect'd him to rage at me at that, but he merely laugh'd and said, in a Tone of the highest Contempt, that nothing I could do could keep him confin'd if he himself wish'd to leave, but that at any rate he would be happy not to be always disturb'd from his Studies by Crackbrains such as I. With that he hand'd over his Key and slamm'd shut his Door.

I had Matthew lock him in and gave him the strictest Instructions. He was not to cease from his Watch on the Door until he be relieved by another, that I would send at Night. It seem'd to me that in this Manner, though I had not the Power to be rid of the Man, I had at least contain'd him where he could do but little Mischief.

We had Wood enough to keep the Fires burning until Christmastide, and a little Gunpowder for the Fumigation of our Chambers. But an ill Wind blew continually across the Towne, and it carried in its Teeth the dread miasmic Stench of foul Corruption. Accordingly, even in College, I was careful not to go about without my Napkin and Pomander. And by degrees I learn'd to hold my Breath, from the Door to the Lodgings as far as Chapel or Hall, or any other Entrance off the Quadrangle. I drank little, and ate Quicksilver, and pray'd for Frost. My greatest Feare was that the Discipline of the House might, in time, be lost. I doubled the Prayers in Chapel, and set out Statutes against Drunkennesse and Vice. 'Twas a strange Relief to have barr'd the Gates and, though we were now on our own, we were at least kept apart from the Evil and Wantonesse and Feare that ruled in the City.

We were then as a Vessel or an Ark, set out brave but lost, upon an Ocean rack'd with a terrible Tempest. Sixty nine there are of us in all, Fellows and Scholars, not counting the dozen Servants, and not one Woman to weaken the Strength of our Resolve. Quinbey the only Uncleanness in our Midst, and he confin'd. I knew that the Fellows and the Scholars all look'd to me for a Lead, and the Weight of that Burden was so great, that I have hardly slept since that Time, and rather pace about my Bed Chamber, and speak to my Image in the Mirror.

But such Sleep I do have is torment'd by dreadful Dreams, (occasion'd no Doubt by the Stories told me by the Mayor, or sent perhaps by dark Forces to agitate my Rest), such as that I go out to Magpie Lane, and visit there a certain House, and commit gross wantonness, and fall asleep, but then I seem to wake up to find that they have put me in the Cart whilst I slumber'd, and I am lying amongst the Bodies of the Dead, and they are all about me and over me and touching me, and I cry out that there is a mistake and that I am not infect'd, at which the Buriers and Beaters do *laugh* at me and say 'Brother, you are now', and do throw me with the rest into that terrible Pit –.

For seven Days and seven Nights we continued in this way, and beyond bad Dreams there was no Disturbance to our Prayers or to our Peace, and the Pestilence was kept out of the College. We lived soberly, ate well, and our Food tasted the better for our Prayers, so that it began to seem that we alone were spared.

We had but little News from the Citie beyond, with the Gates barr'd and Nobodie allow'd to come or go. But there was a Man, a sturdy and a cheerful Fellow, that was a Student of the Queen's College, who appear'd at a high Window every Evening after Dinner, and call'd over to us across the Lane, and gave us what News he could of the Plight of the Towne beyond, and it was grievous News indeed. Besides, in the Stillnesse of the Night we could hear the tolling of the mournful Bells, and the cries of 'Bring out your Dead', and ofttimes distant Screams and Wailings of the Infect'd and those that loved them.

In all this Time we heard Nothing from Quinbey, except when he ask'd for Food. But one morning Hugh Page, who had the Watch on his Door at Night, came to me and said that he had heard strange Noises, and under the Door had seen ghostly and unnatural Lights, and had besides heard Quinbey talking, as if he were not alone, though again he swore that Nobodie had come in to him. He was a simple Man and sorely frighten'd, and talk'd Nonsense of unnatural Powers, so that you might think that he stood guard over Simon Magus himself, or Smerdis, or Zarathustra, or that Solomon and all his Daemons were in wait behind the Door. I told him that Quinbey was ofttimes in the habit of talking to himself, and that whatever infernal Experiments he was conducting, they could do nothing to harm us, which I pray'd was true.

It seem'd, though, that in this I was sorely mistaken. For the man of Queen's, when he call'd across to us that Day, ask'd whether we had been stricken, as their College had been, with the Infection, for he had seen a Plague Doctor that Night passing down the Lane betwixt the Colleges, coming it would seem from us. This I said was impossible, but it troubled me sorely.

That Night (for I knew I should never sleep), I resolved to stay up and keep a Watch upon the Lane. I sat at the High Windows at the Corner, hard over by All Souls' College, which do give the clearest Views.

Some time after the Bells struck Three a Light appear'd in a Window of the Queen's College, and was held up seven times, and then put out. A few minutes later a black Figure in a Cloak, wearing the dread Masque of the Plague Doctor, appear'd in the Lane and walk'd up it towards my End. I could swear to it, though, that he had not come all the way from St Edmund's Hall, so that he must have come either from Queen's or from our side, over the Wall (the Postern Gate of course being lock'd up and barr'd). I immediately hurried to Quinbey's Chambers. Hugh swore that the Door was never open nor unlock'd, and that he had never once slumber'd or left off his Watch. Under the Door there was Light from Quinbey's Candles, and he could be heard at Work, and pacing up and down. At this I was reassur'd, but told Hugh to stay alert, for I was sure that there was no Good in any of this.

The next Day the Sky at Dawn was Dead and Grey, without Variation or Colour, and the Ayre very heavy and close. The Wind, which had look'd to change to the North, where it might blow fresh Ayre from the fields, had swung round again to the Sou'West, and blew in a miasmic Stink from the Town, and then died away altogether, so that the Ayre press'd down upon us most heavily. Towards Noon a light dew began to Fall, and then by Degrees a steady Rain, so that it was all the Servants could do to keep alight the Fires at the Corners of the Quadrangle. That Evening there was no Sign of the Queen's man, and this oppress'd us mightily, for we knew that there could be only one Reason for that.

Nor had there been either Traffic or People in the Lane, nor any Sound from the Town. It was as though the entire Citie were dead and we at last alone. I burn'd to know what had happen'd beyond our Walls, since now we had no more News. A terrible Feare and Oppression bore down on me, and I felt like a Madman, or like an Animal caught in a trap, that waits helpless for its Fate.

That Night I took up Watch again by the very same corner Window. And indeed, at some short Time after Three, there was a Light in the Window in Queen's. Within a few moments the awful Figure of the Plague Doctor again appear'd, coming clearly from our College. At this I must have fairly lost my Wits. Was this Apparition Truth or Vision? And indeed, does it matter if it be real or no – I saw it! And, if seen, might it not also be touch'd? And if touch'd, might its Evil not be suffer'd?

Overwhelm'd with Anxiety, and exhaust'd with Feare and Want of Sleep and not knowing what occurr'd, or what its End would be, and being besides most desirous to know the State of the Citie – for we had heard no News – (and indeed 'twas unknown whether they yet carried on their Trade in Magpie Lane, or were all dead) God forgive me I could not help myself, but I determined at once to follow him. This I knew I might do, since he had still to walk up the Lane, and round the Corner to the Part of the Lane where is the College Gate, which I might reach first and there intercept him, venturing no more than a few Yards beyond the Walls.

I seized my Cloak, and wrapp'd my Mouth and Nose about with Cloth, and took a heavy Bastinade, so that I might keep at Bay any one of the Infect'd if they came near me, though indeed, it seem'd there would be none Abroad, as it was very late, and a horrible foul Night for

Wind and Rain. The Lane was empty and desolate. He had somehow reach'd the far End of it already, and was turning the Corner by the time I rush'd out, and I had to hurry to keep him in Sight, for I was desperate to know the Truth, though I dared not approach him too close, arm'd though I was. And as I follow'd him there came into my Mind those Words of the Psalms, which speak of 'the Pestilence that walketh in Darkness'.

It was then, as I pass'd out of the melancholy Lane into the desolate Streets of the Citie, that I saw the Worst of it, for the Streets were full of fearful Objects. All of them were fill'd with Rubbish and Household-Chattels, and stew'd with Dead Rats and other Animals, which made an insupportable Stench. This was by no means the Worst, for it seem'd that the Death-cart, which it had been my chief Feare of encountering, had not come by this Part for some little Time. Or perhaps it no longer came at all, for it appear'd – and I could not swear to it, for I look'd away and did not tarry longer, in Spite of an over-weaning Curiosity – that there were Bodies also exposed outside some Houses where they had been left. And by the Pit in St Giles there was a Heap of what I took at first to be Rubbish, but I soon hurried away, for I fear it was perhaps rather the Dead lying unburied, against all Christian practice. Death it seem'd reign'd in every Corner, and the Citie was become a Charnel House.

The Towne itself was desert'd, for every Familie had either lock'd themselves in for their own Protection, or been shut up as the Infection had visit'd one of their Household, and thus all been lock'd in with the Infect'd, to face an almost certain Death, as was the Law. In Broad Street half the Houses bore the Red Cross on their Doors. The Guards were gone, who were to keep Watch on the

Houses that were shut up, though whether they had fled as the Infect'd were out at Night for Ayre, by the Mayor's Order, or whether the Orders of the Mayor carried yet any Weight, or indeed if he were even still alive himself, I knew not and I know not now.

The Plague Doctor turn'd South down Turl Street, and I follow'd as best I could, though I was loath to do so, coming out by Lincoln's College into the High. There in the distance I could see other Figures. They were a dismal and a fearful Sight, for I suppose these were poore sicke People. They were too far away for their Features to be discern'd, or any Swellings of their Skin, yet by the miserable Way they moved, 'twas clear they were in grievous Agony and Despair, and I knew they would be the Infect'd: cover'd in Sores, and but walking Putrefying Carcasses. One indeed I saw who ran about dancing, singing, laughing – like a Bedlam Lunatick – which was a very dreadful Thing to behold. I kept well away from them, and they, thank God, from me.

The Man in Black went down into Bear Lane. He knock'd seven times on the Door of a House, that was open'd by a crook'd Man, who was also wearing the Apparel of a Plague Doctor. I dared not follow to confront them, but hid beneath the Window, in a pile of stinking Straw, where Rats and Vermin lived, but where I might catch some of the Voices of those inside.

'We are all here, then?' I heard clearly, and then some Talk I could not make out, and Someone cried:

'Have a Care with that!'

Then, distinctly, I heard Quinbey's Voice, raised as was his wont, saying:

'That is a Discourse full of manifest Ignorance and learned Simplicity.'

So I had guess'd correctly, but til now knew not what Loathsomeness they were about, for to this another Voice answer'd him:

'In all the Bodies we have open'd, we see the gangrenous Inflammations in the lower Parts of the Belly, Breast and Neck.'

To which Quinbey replied:

'Remember Sir, as well as the infect'd Humours, Rheum, and Sputum, and the black and yellow Biles and other residua, you must let me have the Eyes.'

'Twas clear they were cutting up the Bodies of the Dead, and collecting the very Substance of the Plague, for the Purpose of who knows what Devilry. Here indeed was Quinbey caught in the very Act of Maleficium – in other Words of Witchcraft!

At this I grew afraid and came away, but then went back again, for I suppose I desired to hear more, and indeed as frighten'd as I was, I was loath to pass again by the Infect'd, that I knew were now betwixt me and the College. But then it came in to my mind that the Invisible College might see me, and do God knows what to me, so I came away again, and fairly ran back to Safety, and beat upon the Gate til I was let in.

'Twas not til then I realised I could go into Quinbey's Chambers, and find out what Horrors lurk'd there, and destroy them. And I could bar also his Window (though whether he climb'd out onto the Roof of the Long Boghouse – or College Privy – and thence down into the Lane, or whether he rather flew out, I know not); so that, by thus preventing his Ingress, we might at least keep his Evile out of the College, and nor could the Fellows take great Exception to it.

But when I came to his Stair, Hugh swore Quinbey was still inside. At this I was sore perplex'd, for 'twas impossible he had return'd before me. Yet there were indeed Noises from within. And when we got down on our Knees and look'd under the Door, there could be seen his Feet and the End of his Gown, away over on the far Side of the Room. Deciding that I must know the Worst of it, I got the Key and unlock'd the Door and enter'd. I heard a Gasp and saw in front of me – not Quinbey but, as I first thought, another Fellow. But then, the Figure turning in surprise as I enter'd, I saw that, though dress'd in Quinbey's Cap and Gown – presumably to appear as Quinbey to any who look'd under the Door when he was abroad – it was indeed: a Woman!

Seeing me, she first gasp'd, then laugh'd, then took off her Cap, and let her long yellow Hair fall down about her Shoulders. Then her lips open'd and she very prettily said:

'It seems I am discover'd!'

By God she was fair to look at, and her Voice full of Warmth and Joy, of which we have had little enough these last Months gone, though there was sufficient Resemblance for it to be clear, as she herself confirm'd, that here was Quinbey's Sister –'

Part 5 – The Invisible College

'The World we inhabit is an error.
Mirrors and fornication are abominable,
for they multiply the number of Mankind.'
The Annihilation of the Rosa Secreta of the
Veiled Heresiach

Late Evening

At this point I was startled by a loud knocking at the door.
This document was indeed a catalogue of horrors. I did
not know that they had even burned books. But in my
excitement I had quite lost track of time. Here was Fisher
to say he is ready for dinner and to ask me to accompany
him to Hall.

A great wind had got up outside and we bent into it as
we walked, our footsteps crunching on the gravel. There
was a long hedge filled with dead leaves up against the
wall of the chapel, and a sudden gust roared along it like
a terrific malignant force.

It was an effort to enjoy the evening's entertainment. At
first even this Exeat feast barely lifted my spirits, though
the hall was decorated with a tree and paper chains and
crackers. I wonder how many Christmas dinners I have
left in me? My soul seems spread so very thin.

Something unpleasant happened to me at high table.
When we sat down to pull the crackers mine seemed to

hold nothing at all. But then I noticed in it a nail paring, and a long spidery body-hair, and a single folded sheet of tissue paper. Unfolding this paper revealed a quote from the Apocrypha:

> *'Yea Corruption cometh on swift-beating wing*
> *to all creatures who now walk in the light.'*

Bewildered, I did my best not to give a reaction. Perhaps it was a miscalculated practical joke? I am sure I only took it so amiss because of last night's unpleasantness. But on the other hand what could it mean? Of a sudden I feel a long way from home, and very alone.

Fisher, sitting next to me, naturally noticed it too, and he was very cross on my behalf. He told me it was doubt-less intended to frighten, and that it was best not to dwell on it. Almost immediately after this, he asked us to excuse him the first course, and disappeared for fully a quarter of an hour. He returned without giving an explanation, and I was hardly reassured.

Another diverting conversation during dinner, though, soon brought me to myself again. Reverend Simmons joined us for the occasion and a jolly affair it was too in the end. Outside it was now blowing a gale ('Who has whistled it up?' joked Simmons). But, with lamps and candles blazing, the hall was a cheering prospect.

I decided to mention to Fisher I had had a rather dis-turbed night. I had guessed he might have something to say about that. Perhaps I might begin to draw him out and discover the source of this strange reticence of his. But if he was unsurprised he did not show it. Schwarzgruber was there and made a good joke about '*the sleep of reason breeds nightmares*'. Fisher made a favourable comparison to the '*horrors of war*'; and I must have looked shocked, for Schwarzgruber, sitting across from me, said:

'You look like you have seen a ghost, Herr James. But tell me, have you ever seen the dead?'

'Me? No no,' I answered. 'Not unless you count that mummified child they keep in Dublin cathedral – a horrid, thin and shrivelled thing they show to frighten tourists.'

Schwarzgruber interrupted me, saying:

'What I meant was something rather more *unheimlich* – how do you say? – uncanny. Do you believe in such things as ghosts, Herr James?'

'Well, I'm not credulous,' I said, 'but I am prepared to consider the evidence and accept it if it satisfies me. We cannot dismiss these things just because we do not like the idea of their being true. Though I doubt you will find many at this table who would not reject that idea outright. What about you, Herbert? You are a man who preaches the power of science. Can anything of us survive our death?'

(For Fisher, sitting next to me was listening most attentively.)

'No I certainly do not believe such things.' He spoke loudly. 'An Historian must deal only with properly corroborated evidence. Though I must admit I did see one once. At Amiens, when I was visiting the Front. He was a chap I knew from my club, who was a Lieutenant in the Ox' and Buck's. He walked across the road and I waved at him but . . .'

'I suppose you're going to tell us –'

'Yes – he'd caught it up at Loos three weeks earlier. A nasty death, I had heard. They never found enough of him to bury. I only mean to say I don't believe it was a ghost. Just a moment of mistaken identity. I shouldn't have thought twice about it. Nor even remembered it. Not if I hadn't read just after of the poor fellow's death. It was pure coincidence. It doesn't keep me awake at night.'

'That makes sense.'

'I believe there are logical explanations behind all these silly stories,' he continued, glancing at Schwarzgruber. 'They are either hoaxes – and you would be surprised how common they are; or misinterpretations; or stories that have grown in the telling.'

'Misinterpretations?' someone prompted.

'Yes. A scientist would argue that we have *evolved* to see figures and faces. Even when there aren't any there. After all, that is better for us than not seeing them in time when they are. He might justly add that there could be certain forces of electro-magnetism, perhaps not yet fully understood, which might affect some of us in such a way as to cause reactions, which people have misinterpreted as supernatural.'

Here Schwarzgruber spoke up:

'And perhaps psychological factors are also at work. Doctor Freud has argued that persistent morbid dread may signify repressed sexual desires . . .'

'Thank you Dr Freud,' I said, 'but my 'unconscious mind' is a labyrinth that I have no wish to penetrate. In fact I believe that such delving is dangerous. Why dredge up the primitive and sub-human? If Love and Art spring from the 'repression' of animal instincts, then what is so wrong with repression? That is the problem with soul searching – you never know what you might find. And as for the 'interpretation of dreams', I don't believe my dreams make any sense at all. All the same, they are really not so very nice. And I find I cannot help but believe in anything when I am in bed.'

'But I forget myself, Herr James, for have I not read with great pleasure your own charming stories of the supernatural? The stone with seven eyes? How did you get this fascinating idea? And I remember one called '*A Warning to the Curious*'. So amusing. That conceit of the local superstition of the three crowns, buried in the Dark Ages to guard the coast from the Germans, and protected by the ghost who haunts the archaeologist who finds them. Although, of course, you omit to mention that this device cannot have worked in the first place. For as you know the Eastern approaches were unprotected after all. And the Saxon armies conquered your great island in the end. We forget all too easily, I think, the racial unity of our two nations. But we have our own stories, of course. As a child my mother used to frighten us to bed with the tales of the brothers Grimm. Do you know them?'

'Personally I always preferred Christian Andersen,' I replied, suddenly remembering, 'for he is somewhat less dark. As for my own stories, I aim for a pleasing terror, with nothing that is too gruesome. And I don't drag in sex. Sex is tiresome enough in novels. In a ghost story it is a fatal mistake.'

Here we made a fascinating digression into the folk-lore of colleges and schools. Schwarzgruber mentioned the 'Black Scholar', which he had clearly found out all about.

'Be that as it may,' said Fisher, 'we can all agree that one can spend too long sitting up late in one's study. The springs of causation are subtle. When things go bump in the night I need only think of the great sceptical philosopher David Hume. As you might say, there are more things in his philosophy than are dreamt of in heaven and earth . . .'

Here Reverend Simmons, sitting next to him, interjected:

'But, Warden, it is Hume himself that keeps *me* awake at night. If one follows where he wished to lead us, then are we not all of us lost?'

'I did not mean to attack religion, Reverend, only superstition.'

'Of course,' replied Simmons, 'although Hume also teaches us that the only thing we can trust less than our senses is our reason, and there is I think real terror in that. And besides,' (I was coming to see this was typical Simmons, making it clear he was not offended by cracking a joke) 'if one in a moment of fear were to call upon David Hume, only to see him emerge from a wardrobe, with a pumpkin upon his neck and his head under his arm, what would we say then?' (Much hilarity at this.)

To this Fisher replied:

'I only meant to say that – as President Roosevelt has so eloquently put it – we have nothing to fear but Fear itself.'

'Oh but 'fear itself' is the most frightening thing of all,' said Simmons, 'What can it lead a man to do? Or indeed a People?' Here he turned to Schwarzgruber: 'But what about you, Professor-Doctor? What exactly do you believe?'

Schwarzgruber appeared to think carefully about his answer, which for some reason made a great impression on me:

'I believe the World is governed by relations of *power*. Power between objects, as between men. The only thing that matters is the strength of the Will. And as for unnatural visitations, Reverend, you have not yet said where *you* stand on the possibility of spiritual presences. I personally like to remember what our great philosopher Herr

Nietzsche said: '*If you look too deeply into the abyss, the abyss may look back into you*'.'

'Well if we are serious for a moment,' said Simmons, 'I believe that talk of harmless human ghosts is one thing. But it is the idea there might be other, more dangerous, entities out there, that I find to be a renunciation of all that I hold most sacred. The problem of Evil is a fine theological dispute. We must allow the necessity of free will – and hence evil – to all God's human creations. But I can see no way of reconciling the existence of other evil elsewhere in His universe, in other – less human – forms. So it is not the Dead that frighten me – it is the Living.'

'Quite so,' said Fisher, turning on Schwarzgruber, 'and in any case, if '*God is Dead*', then there is surely no such thing as Hell.'

'Forgive me, Warden, but that does not follow. Show me the syllogism that proves that the existence of devils necessarily implies the existence of God. Of all the fascinating things about the Jewish and Mohammedan Demons, the most disturbing, to my mind, is that we are assured that some of them were atheists. Those subtle authors who wrote of such things did not assume that they were a necessary part of a more reassuring cosmology. They cannot be, in fact, for they are pre-Christian syncreses. In other words – and this too is obvious when you think about it for a moment – one can easily believe in the Devil without believing in God.'

At this Fisher sat back heavily in his chair. Schwarzgruber then continued:

'And we may go further. The evidence is all around us. Just think of the enormous cruelties of Nature. They are what drove Darwin to lose his Faith in God. (It was the grubs of the ichneumon wasp, I believe, that eat their living victims from the inside out.) Or consider for a moment the crushing miseries of Man. The vast agonies that we suffer, and inflict – on each other and on ourselves. We always have glimpses of happiness, only for those hopes to be crushed. That could be a part of our torture, no? So perhaps it was the Devil who made this world of ours. Perhaps we are already in Hell.'

There was a sharp intake of breath at this, which even Schwarzgruber noticed. Fisher was awkward and uneasy, and he broke in most assertively with something like:

'I have heard, Herr Schwarzgruber, that at least one member of your government has advocated fornication under pagan stone monoliths, and on the barrows of dead Thuringian warriors. He actually believes this will supernaturally channel the forces of what he terms the 'Master-race'?!'

He meant Mr Himmler of course. There was now an awkward pause.

'Ach so, Warden. So I have heard also' said Schwarzgruber quietly, and then he shot straight back with: 'And the party salute is copied from the Order of the Golden Dawn – ah but that is an *English* occult organisation. It was founded, I believe, by a member of your old University, Mr James. I wonder what he learned while he was there?'

This reference to Crowley silenced us for a moment, and Schwarzgruber continued:

'Ignorance and foolishness are everywhere these days, no? I need hardly say how embarrassed I am, gentlemen, by the current political arrangements in my homeland. Credulity and stupidity are the curse of every nation, sad to say, not least my own. We scholars must work all the harder to protect the truth.'

'Hear hear!' I said, and I was glad when Fisher called grace.

Schwarzgruber had given an elegant reminder of how lucky we are, for we live in a country where we need not profess party allegiance. Though Fisher could now barely conceal his dislike of the man. I talked to him further over a nice tawny port in the SCR. He could see how exhausted I was and sent me to bed, with promises to speak at proper length in the morning. The gale still howls outside. The wind is juddering the window frames against the stonework, and branches of ivy are scratching against the panes. It will be a noisy night.

I to bed, with the wise words of Fisher and Simmons in my ears. If the apparition of David Hume should appear with a pumpkin, I shall ask him in for a cup of tea and speak to him in the sternest terms.

However, in all the excitements of the day I'd almost forgotten about the show-stone. And now I think there will be no harm if I do move it to a cupboard in the outer study. Idiotic it may be but it will help me sleep the better. Fisher is right, I suppose, that nightmares are formed from our fears. And those in the last moments before sleep may be especially potent. I shall deliberately focus on happier reflections. That is not so easy a task as it once was. I feel – what was it the Bard says? – '*As if there is some monster in my thought – too hideous to be shown*'.

There, the job is done and the mirror is hidden away (though I somehow wish I had not again glanced into it). I do feel as if I can almost *hear* it. Anyway – I have smothered it with some old jerseys. As I do so I remember that they do that in the Balkans, with every the mirror that they have, when someone in the house has died. Oh dear,

I wish I had not thought of that. Tonight I think I may allow myself to keep a light on in my bedroom.

4 a.m.

It will not do. *It will not do.* I have not had such a dreadful dream since I was a child at Livermere. So vivid. So grotesque. The curious effect again is of the different layers of sleep.

One moment one is fitfully asleep, dreaming of some horrors: a ticking clock that stopped and then began to run backwards, a baby lying in a ring of roses, with a cockroach crawling across it, and other such unpleasantness that I neither can nor care to recall. The next one is aware of being in a vast space. I realise from the piers that it is Cologne cathedral. But it is plunged in darkness and I am alone. In fact it is so dark that I cannot see the vault above me. Yet I can see a small black sphere before me, suspended just above head height. It is humming with life and I realise it is spinning. As I approach it I somehow know that it is not what it appears (a sphere), but rather it is the Chiliagon – a figure with a thousand sides. I become aware of some very disturbing 'noises off'. Next there is movement on the far side of the building. From the nave I see a black figure wearing a grotesque mask. It is impossible but he is also hovering: floating a yard above the floor. Now he is half-dancing towards me. Then suddenly from the Chiliagon there erupts a deafening noise.

With a start one wakes up – or *appears* to wake up – safely in one's bed, and with the comforting surroundings of one's own room, and with every detail as it should be. Except that for some reason the window is open and – there! – that dark and legless figure is *creeping* through it so oddly and dropping down out of sight onto the floor. How horrible in such circumstances to be unable to move – to be in effect paralysed – struggling helplessly against the sheets. To know that one is dreaming but only then – at the very last moment before the crisis – to be able to wake up.

In one's room again.

But *now comes the true horror*.

For there is a distressing sound of . . . something . . . that drags itself across the floor – coming ever closer – until I can see who – or rather what – it is (for I think it is no trouble to recognise the thing that was the younger Harwood brother, even after all these years, even though there were no eyelids or lower jaw). And then finally a third time I force myself to look – I am *still* dreaming. And this time is the worst of all. It is little Harry Landscombe, at that cherubic age when I first taught him (how well I recall caning him until he was raw), pulling himself up the sheets onto my bed. He seems young and whole and pure. But then his lips curl into a dreadful helpless smile and he raises his hands – and I see that his bowels are spilling out through a great clean gash across his Belly, to which he points as if in *extispicium* until – and knowing one is still asleep but finding it near impossible to wake – one has to force open one's own eyes to see no more.

There! I must have actually done it. For as I write my reflection shows me my eyelids are covered with scratches. And I must have awoken from very deep sleep indeed. For despite my terror I am so riddled with sleep that it is the hardest thing in the world to force myself up. Anything not to drop off again – straight back into the arms of the anathema.

At last I am truly awake. But what is this? The side lights are off. I am sure I had left them on. I reach for the switch but the blessed thing won't work. A problem with the meter? No – the entire building is in darkness. A major fuse must have blown. Or perhaps the gale has cut the power. I stagger up and out into the study to find a candle. In my terror I actually cry out:

'Enough! I no longer wish to see you in my dreams!'

Pray God I do not come to regret the wording of that plea.

There are things underfoot in the dark. Was that a brushing against my leg? It is pitch black and the room is unfamiliar. I reach out and touch the dressing table, and run my hand along it for a match. I feel my watch. Then a vase with flowers. Then I touch something that I cannot figure out. At first I recoil with shock, but it does not seem to move. Panic is not like pain: you can sometimes force it away with an act of will. And to panic now in the dark would be unbearable. So, calming my fears I reach for it again. Is it something hairy? *Crouching?* Suddenly now it does move, rising up at me – it is something alive! – or worse . . . I cry out and stagger backwards, begging it to be Mr Ockham. I hear a noise. There is something else here with me in the room!

There are some very dreadful moments as I find a matchbox. The first match breaks. At last I strike a flame. I am now alone. But I see the study is disarrayed! Their are drawers open and books flown off their shelves. Could I have left it in this state? Surely someone was in here – here in my rooms! But who was it? And why? To frighten me? To search the place? Or is this evidence of something *worse*? Then from the oratory I hear another noise. A draught blows out my match. This is too much

for me and I become quite like a child. I scream out
loud:

'Who's there?!'

There is a scuffing at the door. Thank God! It is Fisher
– with an oil lamp. He bursts in and cries:

'*Where is the mirror?!*'

I show him where it is hidden under the old clothes in the
cupboard and he is mightily relieved. We sit down at my
desk with the mirror set up between us. For several long
and breathless minutes we are silent. I now suspect he too
has felt its power.

'We must destroy it,' say I.

'We must *not* destroy it,' he says firmly.

'You're right – it may have even crueller ways to save
itself from destruction. But Herbert, who could stand such
dreadful dreams?!'

'Dreams? I did not think a man like you would be
frightened by such things. He was surely right who said
misery acquaints a man with strange bedfellows'. But
night terrors cannot hurt you. And seven years of ill luck
might be nothing to the consequences of breaking this
mirror.'

'This is no longer a game. You cannot tell me that the
dream I have just had was natural.'

'Of course it was natural. It is not this mirror that is
plaguing you, but your own mind.'

'But here is proof!' I said, pointing around the room:
'Physical proof in the World of Matter!'

These were clearly hard concessions for a scientifi-
cally-minded man. He now answered:

'Proof? What proof? It only proves someone is trying
to frighten us off, that is all. I suspect they got in through

the oratory window, which does not have a lock. No doubt they hoped to get the mirror for themselves. We must not allow them to succeed. A pity I didn't catch them red-handed. But things have gone far enough. We intend to take action today. I cannot tell you any more at present. Perhaps I should never have got you involved in this. I am sorry for that, Monty, truly I am. But you have played your part admirably well. And do not think we are living in one of your foolish stories. There are forces abroad in the World which are much darker than the quaint spectres of your writings, and very soon now we may have to confront them.'

Fisher would say no more on the subject. But he is good enough to sit up with me now until dawn. Mr Ockham, who is terribly upset, finally comes down from the top of the bookshelves, but he will not suffer me to stroke him. I sit here lost in thoughts about myself. I approach something like calm as, outside, the wind falls, and the sky at last begins to lighten.

December 4th

Morning

The lawns are strewn with debris from last night's storm, but now finally all is still. I shall not spend another night here. If someone or something does not want me here I shall be very happy to oblige them. I have already been through most of Chapman's papers, to little avail. I should be able to finish them off this morning. Then I shall tell Fisher I have had enough, and take myself back off by an afternoon train. If this experience has taught me nothing else it has given me another rule for my stories: real people get out at the first sign something is wrong.

I tried to pray this morning, but it felt forced and somewhat pointless. I have always thought this antiquarian delving could be dangerous. Too often it leads one away from the light of the gospels. Leads one to areas which are enthralling, but troubling – even forbidden, like those that came to obsess John Dee. Sometimes what it brings up can undermine the strongest faith. Perhaps I may have allowed it to challenge mine. And to think: if I had never read the apocrypha as a child I would probably have been a churchman like my father. I suppose you could say I was tempted from that path by this interest in the arcane and occluded. Well I have that to thank for my academic career. But was it not the very same thing that led me away from God?

I feel myself curiously detached from the world. It is as if the laws of Nature have been altered and become malign. Or rather that my eyes have opened and I see they were malign all along. Reality, seen like this, no longer seems as real as my dreams. And my dreams – such dreams! – now haunt me in the waking world. They watch me (or the memory of them watches me), to make sure I take no comfort from human company. I feel like a man who has committed a monstrous crime, and waits – in dread and longing – for the moment of arrest. I do not think I will be happy until I am safely back at Eton.

Still, I should dearly like to solve this riddle before I go. As soon as it is light I shall return once more to Chapman's rooms. That it is not the last place I wish to be, it will not easily be supposed.

And it turns out I was right to wish to avoid it.

I should start by saying that – in the course of the next few horrible hours – I experienced none of the disturbances or noises that plagued me yesterday. In myself, though, I did not feel well. Your health leaves you suddenly, like a sound you hadn't realised you were hearing, but, once stilled, you remember was a roar.

For many months I have been troubled by one ailment or another. But over the last few days things have gone from bad to worse. I have had a series of strange and intense headaches. Other than that there is nothing much that could be described as a symptom when my body is at rest. Instead there is an extreme lethargy and malaise and a feeling of deep unwell. I have begun to have moments where I forget where I am, or what I am supposed to be doing, and it seems to go beyond my normal absent-mindedness.

But now I must relate my grim discovery.

I finished sifting Chapman's notes within two hours. I had found nothing of any use beyond a few more fragments of translation, and those so garbled and corrupt that not much sense could be made of them. Nor could I get any inkling of the source he was trying to translate. It was only as I was reaching the very bottom of the pile that I read something that in an instant pushed all scholarly thoughts aside. In the lower border of one of the last pages of notes, Chapman had drawn an asterisk and written:

'Dreamt again last night of the cryptospeculant.'

I read this over with incredulity, and mounting panic. What did he mean? I turned to the top of the next page, where he had added:

'It was the Plague Doctor again, in a labyrinth of marble. When I seemed to wake up it was in here with me. This time was worse than the others.'

Don't tell me that you too, my dear Chapman, had been assailed by these most repulsive dreams? For God's sake, let that not be true! The shock of this discovery brought on a sudden bout of nausea. It sent me stumbling next door into the bedroom, where I retched into the basin. Then I made myself lie down upon the bed.

But what I had already read in his diary now made more sense. What would Fisher say to this? I may have dreamed it all – but what consolation is that, if I am not the only one to have dreamed it?

At last I begin to have an inkling of what Chapman must have suffered. This is of course the very bed on which he died. What was it he saw that night, at the supreme moment of death? What happened to him in this room that now might be waiting for me?

As I am lying there I look around the room. It is an even more curious shape than the main room it adjoins. It has clearly been carved out of an awkward corner of the building, somewhere between the chimney stack and the stairwell. The internal partition cannot have been intended by the architect, but must have been put in later at a curious angle, in order to make a set of sorts with the odd-shaped study on the other side. It is very dark and cramped.

I was lying on the bed recovering from my sickness, and wondering vaguely about how difficult they must have found it to fit in the furniture. That is when I saw it. Or rather I saw a corner of it. It was only visible from my position on the bed, and only just from there. Not even the Scout could have noticed it.

There was a slight angle in the partition, which prevented the bed-side drawers from lying quite flush against the wall. Into this angle between this chest and the plasterwork there was something stuffed down as far as it would go. I tried to reach into the gap but it was too small, and I never fancy putting my hand somewhere I cannot see. Instead I sat up and dragged the heavy piece forward, until I could see clearly behind it. The gap revealed a small sickly yellow ball (that must have been a nest of spiders' eggs), a thick string of dust, a farthing, and – leaning against the wall: a book.

It was a large flat folio, bound, I should say, in the sixteen hundreds, and also stuffed with sheets of modern paper covered in Chapman's notes. Seizing it I felt a leap of excitement in my chest. It has not been printed – the whole book is written by hand. I opened it at the frontispiece – a field of cabbalistic symbols, at the centre of which appear the following words:

'Liber Mysteriorum Sextus

et

Speculum Metus
Johannes Dee, MDLXXXIII

This Booke is a Mirror, in which ye may read the Wisdome of the Angels, and see reflected all the Fears, Desires, & Trespasses of thy Soul . . .'

My God – it is the missing book of Dee. O quae deliciae! So you had it all along, Chapman, you old dog! Why on Earth did you hide it? Had you got an idea of the value of this discovery, and were you determined to keep it for yourself? No, that thought is unworthy of me. Did you fear, perhaps, that someone else would take it? Yes I am sure that must be it. But who? And why?

So here is Dee's Sixth Book of Mystery. The volume of wisdom so jealously-guarded that he only ever made a single copy. The learning that may explain and solve all the secrets of his other work. The book that may allow me to publish the greatest find in this field for a generation! How fitting that it should have disappeared only to appear again like this. What a wonderful opportunity for me to end my academic career with a triumph.

If I could prove once and for all that Dee was no naïve frustrated scholar who, impatient for deeper knowledge, was taken in by a parasitic conman. If I could reveal instead the workings of a great and sinister mind, attempting of his own volition the darkest and most forbidden forms of magic . . .

But before I allow myself the delicious moment of reading it, I shall first examine the notes that Chapman left inside it. They may explain where he found it, and why he had hid it away.

Midday

Things are – alas! – so much worse than I had feared. I now see all too well what Chapman suffered. How I fear that I shall be next in line.

These notes contain the missing meat of his researches. From Woodward's text it was clear that the show-stone had originally been purchased by Quinbey, together with a book. A book by John Dee of great necromantic learning: part coded instruction manual, part diary of use. The book now in my hands. For some reason this association between the book and the mirror was lost – perhaps after the last War. But the College had retained both items in their ramshackle collection. It seems they did not even know they had it. Once Chapman knew what he was looking for he had spent hours rummaging in the archives and the treasury. He had eventually found it, piled up with some account books from the period, in a large wooden bureau in the Muniment Tower.

The effect this had had on Chapman can easily be imagined. There was an obvious sense of triumph in his initial description of the find, followed by increasingly breathless notes recording his progress through the book. But alongside his growing excitement, it seemed, there began to creep in the first signs of fear. His notes recorded the gradual collapse of his nervous constitution, as he became the victim of a nameless terror – a sort of spectrophobia. The progress of this psychological descent into a hell of his own devising could easily be traced in the pages he had hidden in Dee's book:

'Originally the obsidian may have been volcanic, or fashioned from a large tektite. Long before Quinbey got to it, or Dee himself, it was clearly designed to be a cultic divination tool. That its original use was thus as a *psychomanteum* is surely not without interest.'

'It does not take much imagination to realise *what* they worshipped, and with what appalling rites.'

'Alphonso de Spina states that the number of the fallen was 133,306,668.'

'3 times 3 times 9 is 81. 81 years from Dee's to Quinbey's first use. 10 times 3 times 9 is 270. 1935 minus 1665 is 270. 270 years from Woodward's document to the present day. Does it obey a hidden sequence?'

'Here Dee started to record the date and time of every congress with his wife!'

'Might some mirrors reflect more than light? Might some mirrors not be, perhaps, two-way?'

'Can it really be the spiritualists are right? That the Dead can be contacted by the Living, through objects or words of power? A coin, a cup of wine, a book, *a mirror* – is it possible?'

'I will not be tempted into contact with him – it is obscene.'

'I am misled – there can be no return. It is my own thoughts I see, in dreams.'

'But I sinned only in my mind! Why does this torment me now?'

'The timings are not regular. Why? I can only assume it is a deliberate attempt to heighten the dread. Sampson must have suffered this torture for three years. It will drive me mad.'

'No. No. No. No. No. No. No.'

'Admisi maleficium Bogomilorum et Bestialitatem cum Incubo qui est in speculo.'

'I can only look upon myself with revulsion.'

'But I believe that Woodward saw it too . . .'

'It is true! I am not the first to be afflicted!!! – Bk1, Ch4.iii.'

I immediately looked up the section of Dee's book to which he refers. To my distress, but not my surprise, it is a description of a startling series of dreams. They apparently beset Dee after he first started to use the object. For example:

'I had a Vision that Edward tooketh the Darkenesse and wrapp'd it up, and casteth it into the Middle of the earthen Globe, and then his Eyes turn'd black, and his Head roll'd backward, and he float'd above the Table of Practice and slowly span. And the God that was in the Glasse spake through him, and said that of Hope there was none, nor Meaning neither, nor Mercie.'

'I had a Dream of being naked and my Skyn all over wrought . . . with Crosses blew and red; and on my left Arm, abowt the Arm in a Wreath, these Words I read: 'sine me nihil potestis facere' – 'without me you can do nothing'.'

'I dream'd on Saturday Night that I was dead, and afterwards my Bowels were taken out, and I walk'd and talk'd with divers Men, and among others with the Lord Treasurer, who was come to my House to burn my Books when I was dead.'

After this Chapman's notes become less and less coherent:

'Did I invite this demon in? No. For it seems all those who seek to use the mirror have likewise been afflicted. Perhaps Fisher is right? That these visions . . . manifestations . . . are a sort of side effect, produced by some kind of resonance or power of which this stone is a source. Or are they somehow its way of directing itself to where it wants to be – or defending itself from unsanctioned use? Or is it only those who do not reflect sin who are worthy of wielding its power? I do not think it can be appeased without the 'secret of safe use'.'

'But Fisher has looked into the mirror, and is not affected.'

'I see it now – it is not the mirror, but the book. Would to Christ I had never found it!'

'But they died of natural causes. Unless, perhaps, *some natural deaths are not really natural at all?!*'

'That these things only appear to those in extremis proves nothing. Perhaps you have to be asleep or ill, half-mad or dying, before you can see the ineffable . . .'

'Dreamt of it again last night. *He was in my rooms!* What is it? This unutterable thing. An abomination.'

'Let us call it a *cryptospeculant*. They live in two places, I suppose: in fever dreams and mirrors.'

'If you look for it in the mirror you will never quite see it – it is only as you glance away that you catch it with the tail of your eye. But I know that it is always there. It is almost too horrible to contemplate: if in these monstrous glimpses I can see it then – oh Christ! – we must also assume that *it can see me!*'

Beyond these ravings there is nothing I can bring myself to set down on paper. Here was shocking stuff indeed. It is clear to me now that something must be done – and done quickly – if I am to avert whatever horror overtook Chapman at the end. Overtook Chapman, and perhaps Sampson and others before him. The code attached to the show-stone no doubt contains some intimation as to the forces behind these events. But all my efforts to break it have come to nought. I cannot hope for help from that direction.

Enough! Surely I need not to so abandon myself to despair. For do I not possess the great missing book of Dee? A book written in 1583 by a man who went on to live for another quarter century? A man who, for all his faults, was perhaps no bumbling eccentric, or Cagliostrian impostor after all. A man, indeed, who had at the end provided passages on '*The Secret of Safe Use*'. They may prove to be esoteric, but perhaps they will yield their subtleties up to careful investigation from me. Here, had Chapman only looked for it, would be the secret of how to avert the fate which had come for him – and which is perhaps in danger of coming for me. It was with great eagerness that I now turned to it.

At last I understand Chapman's attempts at translation. For the relevant sections on the 'Secret of Safe Use' are written in Enochian, scrawled out by hand at the end of the book. From the fragments I have already seen, Chapman must also have read it – a painstaking process for him, for he had obviously no previous acquaintance with the language or its script, though for some reason he did not keep a final translation. Here then is the key to the whole. Could it be dangerous to read on? Chapman seemed, if anything, to fear the book more than the showstone. But there is danger, surely, in delving far enough to glimpse a horror, but not deep enough to learn what it is, or how it may be averted. I set myself to reconstructing a translation.

It is a long time since I looked at anything in Enochian. But the letters are not unfamiliar. And Chapman had gathered all the materials I need to attempt a translation – from the *Liber Loagaeth* itself, to a modern reconstruction of an 'Enochian dictionary'. I can now see that he had done much of the work for me. For it was clearly these passages he had been attempting so laboriously to translate – hence the notes I had been working through for days. He has made a few errors, but most of it is sound.

Putting together the phrases he had already done, and filling in as many of the gaps as possible, I can make out the following:

'These words are as a mirror as the mirror on which they were writ. They shall show thee thy fears as thou shalt show thy fears to him. The World in which thou dwelleth is a shattered reflection of the [Heavens?]. Existence and Extension are illusion: they are naught but the shadows of a dream. All [Essence?] is an accident of Power. [ILLEGIBLE] thou canst touch Darkness not, nor canst thou touch Hatred, nor Time, nor Pain – yet by all these thou canst thyself be touched. So thou mayst indeed fear that which lacks Extension[?], for it is not among the necessary qualia of Power.

Words too have power, and these words must be neither read, nor writ, nor spoken. There is but one path to wield this power in safety, but there is no path to wield this power without [propitiation?]. That it should be thus for the [beings of the?] twelfth circle would be impossible, but the Illuders too can [UNKNOWN WORD], and will aid thee, in feats of magnificent power, only payment must be made.

Thou must not read these fatal words, for these words have fatal power.

The seven syllables of power are these:

⟋	*(Gisg)*
⌐	*(Graupha)*
Ɛ	*(Xtall)*
⌐	*(Med)*
⼇	*(Or)*
⼈	(Und)
Ⅴ	*(Pa)*

Thus are revealed the seven keys of the seven gates of the [UNKNOWN WORD] *of the hidden* [Heavens?]. *But once opened they cannot be closed. Thus are revealed the* [UNKNOWN WORD] *of the Four. But to speak these words or write these words or read these words will be as a trumpet clarion to he who waits. He awaketh, he is summoned, he is hungry, and he cometh in the form of thy fears.* [ILLEGIBLE], *without the secret of safe use herein described. What god can save thee now?*

He is already coming.'

And that is all. I am not especially delighted to discover that the tractatus is incomplete. The next two pages have been torn out. Someone at some time must have removed them. But who would have destroyed the very passages which might render this malignant object safe? And what in the name of Christ could it have said?

How I now wish I had left it alone. How foolish of me to read it, in spite of all the warnings. '*Thou must not read these fatal words, for these words have fatal power*'. I begin now at last to understand Chapman's actions. No wonder he destroyed his translation. I suppose this was the point at which he despaired. Whatever arcane and ancient knowledge Dee possessed that allowed him to somehow render the show-stone safe, and whatever 'awful rites' disarm this bizarre curse that unlocks its powers, it seems their description still existed in Woodward's day, but now it has been lost.

Calm, Monty, calm! This is not finished yet: for have you not found an old friend who has already described this book, and who may go on to describe it further? I shall turn for one last time to Warden Woodward, in the forlorn hope that he may yet explain what these missing pages said, or where to find them:

Part 6 – Penetrans Ad Interiora Mortis

'If the doors of perception were cleansed every thing would appear to Man as it is: Infinite.'

The Marriage of Heaven & Hell

'Exhaust'd as I was, I talk'd late with Alice Quinbey in my Lodgings, having brought her out away from that Chamber, with its fearful Apparatus. I ask'd her where her Brother was and what the Devile he was about. She could tell me little of his 'Experiments', of which she claim'd she knew Nothing, as one merely Lodging there for Safety, beyond that she thought them harmless, though even then it were hard enough to believe her in this Matter, for all that I Wished to do so. As for his Whereabouts, she said he had gone out into the Towne to see his Friends, and to gather more Equipment and some Food, and that she had cried and begg'd him not to go, and in that at least I believed her.

I told her it was not safe for her to remain there when Quinbey return'd, he having been outside the College, as he might carry back with him the Infection (I said nothing then of what I knew else). I assured her that, she being now here, I would not send her hence into the Citie, which indeed were Death itself. I invited her to stay in a Room in my Lodgings – a Woman, under my Roof! – who, as she herself said it, was thrown entirely upon my Mercy. After all, she not being infect'd, and a Stowaway, as it were, upon our Barque, it was now our Christian duty to keep her safe, nor could I conceive what else I could do. By God, but she was handsome. She was, besides, so grateful to me, as though I were indeed 'the best of Men' and – as she would have it – 'her Saviour'.

But as for Quinbey, I could not lock him out of the College, as he would call and beat upon the Gates, and it was impossible that neither she nor the other Fellows would not hear it. I resolved instead to allow him to return into his Chambers, and there confront him with his Misdemeanours, and put it to him he had brought with him into College infectious Slimes, and the Eyes of the infect'd Dead, against all Law and Custome, for the Purposes of Goetia and Veneficium (that ancient, foul, and subtle Lore of Poisons), and to confine him there alone away from her, and bar his Window from without, so that he could neither enter the rest of the College nor on the other Hand could he leave it.

He fairly raved when he return'd, and found he was discover'd. He beat against the Door, and howl'd for his Sister. He asked what we did with her, and demand'd she be return'd to him, and threaten'd and cursed us with the evilest Language there is, and sobb'd most unnaturally.

This was no Solution, then, for Alice was by Morning desirous of returning to him, or at least to go and speak with him through the Door. And she could not see what Reason I could have to dissuade her. She had a forceful Way with her, so that it was impossible to doubt that her gentlest Suggestions would not be carry'd out. She intimated that she loved him dear enough, and said he was not the same as other Men, but rather like a Child, who need'd constant Succour.

I could by no means allow her to see him, lest he cast some Diabolick spell, or turn her against us. I told her he had not return'd, and must have seen he was discover'd, and must now be staying Elsewhere with his Friends. At this she sobb'd fit to break, which was grievous to behold – though I tried to comfort her with my Embracings – after which she ask'd to return to his Chambers, so that she at least could wait for him there. But this of course I could in no ways allow, he being return'd when I had told her he was not, and with a Story to tell that would be so different from my own. Yet I could not think on what Grounds to forbid it.

Accordingly I told the Servants to go immediately and fetch out Quinbey, when the Rest of us were at Hall, and to tell him he was being taken to her, and that she was put up in the Treasury room in the Bell Tower, and to take him thither. But instead when he was got there by this Deceit, they were to throw him by main Force into the Cellar, and lock him in there, and to listen to no Thing he said, nor allow him to go near his Apparatus, he being a Witch and Necromancer. Indeed it seem'd the only safe Course to take for the present Time, as here was one who carried the Means of spreading the Infection, and now bore against us a mortal Grudge, as he himself had said.

They did it too, and found him still dress'd in his Devilish Apparel, quite beside himself with Rage. They report'd that he had raved like a Man possess'd when he saw what they were about, and had spoken terrible Threats and Curses against them and me, and that they had struggled with him greatly, and bloodied him, and broken his Arm, and flung him down there – into that Oubliette – into that dreadful Darknesse – alone.

Alice was sore vex'd at her Brother's disappearance, and could barely be consoled for several Days. She often said she would herself have gone out into the Town, had she but known where he was gone. During this Time I often walk'd abroad with her about the College and the Gardens, and, as I thought, we grew in each other's Affections, I now being her Protector, as she was wont to call me, since her Brother had not return'd. For this she did not seem to blame him. She said it was like him, and one of his strange Ways, but she fear'd for him. She seem'd to take Succour when I said that I was sure his Friends look'd after him, and that he was doubtless closer by than she could guess. 'Twas a strange Thought indeed to walk with her around the Cloisters, and to listen to her talk and laugh, and admire the Smoothness of her Skin, and the Lustre of her Hair, and know all the while her Brother was in the Darkenesse there below us.

It seem'd that God, in the darkest Nights of our Despair, had sent to me at last the loving Light of Hope. Alice said, in her strange Way of talking, that she thought of me as dark blue, this being a Conceit of hers, that she forms an Association of Ideas betwixt her Senses, so that she claims to see Colours when she converses or hears Music, of which perhaps I should have taken more Note when she told me, as it is hardly the way of Nature.

She had a quick Intelligence, and was not unacquaint'd by their Parents with all the Accomplishments of Education, although she had (no doubt from her Father) a foolish Preference for the later Followers of Plato. She was one, so it seem'd, like myself, who loved the Words of the divine Poet Milton, and when once I ask'd her how she felt in her Heart, she spoke aloud that Verse in which he says:

'Receive thy new Possessor, one who brings
A Mind not to be changed by Place, or Time.
The Mind is its own Place, and in itself
Can make a Heaven of Hell, a Hell of Heaven.'

which, in Truth, gave me great Pleasure to hear, and seem'd most suitable to our Plight, though, as I now think on it, that Verse is one put in the Mouth of Satan.

She had read Augustine too, and Boethius, and a Translation of the Metaphysics, and was besides familiar with several of the Arguments for the Existence of the Almighty, so that she had some learning in Philosophy in Despite of her Sex, and as it seem'd she prettily consent'd to seek further Instruction from me. Last Friday we talk'd of Oxford in the Future, when the Pestilence was gone, though she would not suffer me to take her Hand in mine.

Meantime, though she knew it not, I had contain'd my Enemie her Brother, and intend'd to keep him confin'd til we were safe. But it came by degrees to my mind that even this was not enough. There was but little Safety with Quinbey yet living, lest he direct on us who knows what Forces of Darkenesse. And would not his Confederates – the Living or the Damn'd – seek his release? Or might not the other Fellows discover his Fate, and take Pitie upon him, to the Danger of the College and the Death of my Authoritie? (For my Position, with them as with his Sister, was by no means yet Secure, and it must be certain, as he himself had threaten'd me, that he would never let her speak to me again on his Release.) And was it not indeed a Crime, to be the very Means of Sustenance for such a Man? Better surely to leave his Fate to God, who judges us all. I order'd the Servants to offer him no Food or Keep, nor to open for any Reason the Hatch into the Cellar.

All this while I was careful to be most attentive to Alice, and to begin by slow degrees to win her Trust and Gratitude. She was all Dignity and Grace, or so it seem'd, and God forgive me I had thought she had conceived an Affection for me, which I now see was but a Device, though it seem'd real enough to me then, and I can scarce believe even now there was not some Truth in it. She at last agreed to give me a Locke of her beautiful yellow Hair, to shew her Favour towards me, which did please me greatly (for I had ask'd her for it often), and which lately I was wont to press against my face, and keep ever close to me in my Chamber.

At Night (for still I could not sleep) I would discourse with my reflection in the Looking-Glasse, and it came into my Mind that there were stranger things than that I might win her, young and comely though she was, and the Daughter of a Gentleman. She was, after all, under the Power of my Authoritie, albeit I was careful to obey all the Degrees and Modes of Courtship. In that the Going was slow enough. For every Step I took toward my Goal I had to overcome much wilful Misunderstanding, much playful Resistance, as if she was but toying with me, or making Time whilst she wait'd for her Brother to return, or for the Frost to come and the Distempter to abate, or for Heav'n alone knows what.

Her Neck was very pretty, though she had a Mole upon it, that I did not like, but this at most Times cover'd by her lustrous Hair. Her Voice was soft and full of Wit. If she thought she said something that displeased me, she would lay her Hand against my Arm, and teasingly ask for my Forgiveness.

Once, as we were sat upon the Mound, I begg'd her to let me kiss her. She was startled and laugh'd at me and shook her Head, though then when she saw I was serious she affect'd to pitie me, and told me that it would not be right at such a Time, and that she was sure her Brother would not like it. At this I ask'd again and, taking my Courage in my Hands, made as to kiss her, and she cried out and pull'd away from me and left me where I was, alone.

Beneath the Bell Tower Quinbey had neither Food nor Water (beyond whatever Dampness was in the place), nor Light nor Warmth, besides being injured and bloody, and the Servants thought he must be extending his Life unnaturally by some Witchcraft, or by the catching and eating of Vermin.

When on the seventh Day he could no longer be heard ranting and cursing, I went to the Bell Tower and stood by the Hatch to the Cellar and call'd gently out to him. A faint horse Voice replied thus:

'By what Right, Warden, am I confin'd in this wretched Place?'

'By Right of my Authoritie,' said I, 'and as Punishment for your many Diabolical Wrongs. For I have discover'd in you the most infamous Necromancie in Oxford since the Days of Roger Bacon. But you shall not prevail – I will have Order in this College.'

'Order?' he raged, 'Order? For this you have buried me alive? Cut out this Stone of Madness from your Brain!'

'Not mad, Sir – never mad. Not I.'

'Then I beg you in the Bowels of Christ – Will you not

at least bring me some Water, and my Papers, and for the Love of God some Light?!'

'That you might use them to cast a Curse? Indeed no. For I have had them burn'd.'

At this there was a low Groan.

'And my Sister?' said he, 'Is she at least safe? Our Parents are both dead – she is my Ward.'

'She is my Ward now, Sir.'

'She shall never speak with you again, when she discovers this,' he said.

'Indeed? But you shall remain there undiscover'd.'

'But I know how the Distemper is spread!' he cried. 'So Great a Death from a Thing so Small – such great Effect from such a tiny Cause. Devile take you, Sir! – see you not? – you would bring the Evil upon you all if you do not for God's sake let me out!'

Which seem'd to me as good as a Confession, so that my Suspicions were thereby confirm'd.

'Well you can do no more of your Mischief down there.'

To which he replied, in a most sarcastic and despairing Manner:

'And to think I was approach'd so near. See what you have done! Indeed 'tis true: 'Manners makyth Man'!'

At that I left him, and would listen to his Cries no more.

But then all my Fortunes were most cruelly dash'd. Hugh – damn his Eyes – who had pitie for Quinbey, and perhaps more than Pitie for Alice, did blurt to her that her Brother was not outside the College at all, and that I might know Something of it. And when I denied this and would not tell her, she raged at me and cursed and scratch'd me, and said she hated me, and that she would make me sorry for it, and became like an Animal in her

Wrath. She went back to Quinbey's Room, and would not open the Door to me, whatever loving Words I spoke to her, and laugh'd at me, and ask'd how I could think she would ever be mine. I ofttimes return'd to her door that Day, sometimes to entreat her, sometimes just to sit Watch outside it, but she swore she would never more speak with me until I told her what was done with her Brother. It seem'd I would have no Choice but to take her to him. I fear'd this most of all, for what would he say to her on his Release? And what Reason could I give, that would not make her hate me?

But that same Day, towards Evening, they came to tell me they had heard no further Noises for many Hours. I had them wait one more Night, then open up the Cellar. Quinbey was lying in the far Corner. Upon his Face was a terrible Expression of Rage and Feare. He was quite dead. The College was free at last from his Foulness. Every Wall and Surface in the Place they said was cover'd with Symbols and numerical Scrawlings, and Pictures of Eyes, and obscure Writings, written in his own Blood and Filth. I told them on no Account to read them but rather to wash them all away, and to bury him un-consecrated in the Earth, that the College at last might be clean.

This was Wednesday – two days ago – the Day the great Frost arrived at last, and we thought to be saved. We allow'd ourselves a Feast that Night in Hall, with a Grace Cup brought by the Butler to the Steward, who got out of his Place and came to my Chair and drank to me out of it, and gave thanks for all I had done, wishing me besides a merry Christmas. I then did take it of him and drank also, wishing him the same, and then it went round, three standing up all the time, and from the High Table it went down to the Bachelors and Scholars, and all did

149

drink, and all applaud'd me, though I was melancholick enough in my Heart, with the thought I could never now have Alice. Nor will she let it alone, but will be asking others after her Brother. It is enough to make me mad.

That Night at last I slept a little, but very fitfully, and had at once a Sweat and a Chill, and my Sleep was disturb'd by the most dreadful noisesome and choking Dreams. Three times he walked around the Cloisters, *backwards*. It was Quinbey, dress'd still in his Plague Doctor's Apparell. Then he stood under the Yew Tree and pointed up at my Window and bark'd.

In my Dream Alice then came to my chamber, and she stood – like an Angel – and was naked, with her long yellow Hair loosed about her Face, and a copper Band about her Throat. I call'd her to me, but when she came over and I push'd back the Confusion of her Hair from before her Face – it was Quinbey! – and he had no Eyes – and he moan'd and touch'd my Neck.

I awoke in terror feeling most dreadful sicke throughout my whole Bodie, with a horrid insolent Pain upon my Neck, and in the Pits of my Arms, and there was Everywhere a fearful Brightness that hurt my Eyes. May God have mercy on my Soul! I call'd in Matthew, and he brought the Chaplain. But they would not come near me. In their Faces I read the awful Truth. When I shout'd to them:

'What is it, Man?!'

They could not look me in the Eye, and could only say:

'You know what it is.'

At this I raved at them and told them 'twas nothing but a Fever. And that it was no Token of the Distemper upon my Neck, but only the Outbreak of a Bruise I had from falling against my Table, and many other such Things. But yet they would not even bring me a Lance to break the Buboe.

Nor could I see how it was, that I alone in the College was infect'd, nor how it could serve God's Purpose, that they who were impure should not have it as well as I.

It was then in an Instant, crying to God, that I saw in my Bedclothes the Locke of her Hair. It alone of the Objects I had touch'd could have borne the Infection upon me. Indeed – God forgive me! – I had ofttimes press'd it to my Face, and smell'd it, and kiss'd it, and kept it by me on my Pillow. Yet now I look'd anew, could it be I had seen not its true Shade of Colour, but that I had wish'd to see? Indeed I had never thought til now that it might not be the Hair from her Head. Might it not rather be taken from one dead of the Distemper – that was cut up by the Invisible College – and given me as a Token, not of Love, but of Death?

So now I knew her former Kindnesse to me was no more than the dissembling Appearance of Affection, and not the Thing itself. In that moment I saw clearly and distinctly that it was she who had cursed me with the Plague, and that she as well as her Brother was a Witch.

I sent away the Chaplain, for his mumbling Ministries were as Torture as the Pain of the Swellings. Then I took myself the Holy Book, and open'd it, and came almost at once, as if an Angel guided me, to the Verse of Exodus, that says:

> 'For I will at this Time send all my Plagues upon
>   thine Heart,
> and upon thy Servants, and upon thy People;
> that thou mayest know that there is None like me
>   in all the Earth.
> For now I will stretch out my Hand, that I may
>   smite thee
> and thy People with Pestilence; and thou shalt be
>   cut off from the Earth.'

In an Instant I knew what I must do, before I grew too weak with Delerium and Pain (and indeed it fair took the Last of my Strength to return and dictate this Warning to Posteritie, so that I think it is the last Thing I do upon this Earth) and I thank'd God Almighty for making me the Instrument of His Will.

I forced myself up, and rush'd in my Nightclothes from the Chamber into the Quadrangle, where the Brightness of the Sun was so great that it made me sick to my Brain, and I thought I would faint. Some of the Fellows were over by the Hall, and they call'd out to me. It was an Idea at once grotesque and comic, that I was a dead Man in their Midst, and that they should not yet know it.

I went on, with my Eyes half shut against the Light, for I knew the way to Quinbey's room, to where she had retired, and when I got there I forced open the Door. The filthy Slut said nothing to me, but gave me a sneering Look of the haughtiest Disgust and Contempt, and stepp'd away from me. I ran at her, the Whore, and push'd her against the Wall before she knew what I did, and as she scream'd I kiss'd her on the Mouth, and on the Face and on the Neck, til I was sure she had received the fatal Breath. There could be no Doubt that I had sown in her the Eggs of that Corruption that would 'ere long hatch and start to grow. Yet in Spite of all she did not cry, but just lay silent on the Floor, which I take as final Proof she is a Witch. For the rest I had merely to lock her in the Chamber, until the Fires of Hell receive her. 'Twas an Eye for an Eye. Thank the Lord I was able to do this Act of Goodness before the End of my Life, and so perhaps yet save the College, which already sickens.

They come to ask me, through my Chamber Door, where Quinbey is. I tell them I have seen him, walking – yes he walks! – around the Cloisters beneath my Window! But what of that? His Body lies below, and he can do me no more Harm. I have removed and burn'd the last of his Papers, and I have destroy'd those Pages of his Book which contravene the Lord's Commands. Even in the Mirror I can now see clearly the Marks and Tokens of my Death. Is it truly me, the raving Bedlamite, who stares out blackly from the Glass? I must now make ready to face that dread Judgement, for which the Pains and Sorrows of this imperfect World are but a Preparation. Enough! God forgive me. God forgive me. God forgive me.'

Part 7 – A Warning to the Introspective

'I'll break my staff,
Bury it seven fathoms in the earth,
And, deeper than did ever plummet sound,
I'll drown my book.'

Tempest, 5.1

Afternoon

That was the end of the manuscript. Chapman had found nothing more.

All Fisher would say when he had read it was:

'My God! You as well? It was the same story with Chapman. I wasn't sure that you too would succumb to these fears. I am sorry I ever got you involved in this, believe me, but it was vital you acted as you did.'

We were standing now in the oldest portion of the Old College wine cellars, which we had entered from a trapdoor under the Bell-tower. In the beam of our torches we could see hundreds of bottles, covered with layers of dust. Very beautiful they were too: the rhythms of their tenebrous rows, and the promise of what they contained, waiting there in the darkness. Many of their labels were mildewed and peeling in the underground damp. Tiny translucent long-limbed spiders hung motionless amongst them.

I looked up at the hatch above us and contemplated it closing on me for the last time, plunging me into that dungeon darkness. It was not, I must admit, an especially pleasant prospect.

'I am not sure which end is the more unspeakable,' I said: 'the fate of Quinbey or that of his sister. To die of the Plague, or be buried alive?'

'Very nasty, to be sure,' said Fisher. 'I had no idea how bad things in College had been. It is like something from Poe: "*Prince Prospero was happy and dauntless and sagacious. But the Red Death had come – like a thief in the night – and now held dominion over all . . .*" '

There was an awkward silence. Then he added, somewhat absent mindedly: 'These cellars would have been a lot smaller back then, and in those days were not used to store wine. Look at all this Rauzon Séglas: I didn't know we had so many left – 1924 – damned fine year it was too. I knew something terrible had happened in here, but I'll admit I had no idea what . . .'

I sniffed the air. Even with the trap-door open above us, down here it smelled horribly musty.

'Something smells rotten,' I said.

'It is just damp soil,' said Fisher. 'Though I suppose in the end that's what all earth is – the decayed remains of things that were once alive. That is Nature's way.'

I closed my eyes, stretched out my hand, and gave the wall a tentative stroke. The stonework was damp to the touch, and mottled with leprous growths of lichen. In some places roots had come through. Instinctively I pulled my hand back.

'Perhaps evil is created by belief in evil,' said Fisher. 'It seems Quinbey was a legend that made itself true.'

I asked him what he meant by that.

'I mean that Fear is like a virus. It is contagious. I wondered whether, if you knew what Chapman suffered at the last, his fears might also infect you. I see that I was right to think that. For they have clearly done so.

'And it is hardly surprising, is it? He happened to be having a breakdown at the same time as he was delving into some pretty nasty stuff. It is no wonder he became convinced that this mirror was not just a powerful symbol – which is one thing – but that it was protected by some sort of curse – even, at the end, that it had called something up or released it into the College. You read his fears, and became frightened yourself, of the very same thing. And after all, by the sound of it, you both read this book of Dee's – as did Woodward, now that I think of it – and of course you both read this,' (here he waved Woodward's document at me). 'I must confess the parallels are striking, but that doesn't make this mumbo jumbo true. It is clear to me you have all been scaring each other. Don't forget, Monty: dreams are just a sort of metaphor, are they not? And Fear is a dreadful guest we choose to invite into the house of our mind. We must not let it in.'

At this he put his hand on my shoulder and looked me in the face.

'But if you had seen what I have . . .' I said, and I am ashamed to say my voice caught in my throat.

At this he released his grip. He sighed, lent back against the wall of the cellar, and said:

'Did you wonder where I'd gone last night? After that business with the cracker I determined that enough was enough. I got Martin up out of the Porters' lodge and we went and searched Schwarzgruber's rooms. And what do you think we found? A detailed map of the College, covered in notes, and a copy of the keys to the Chapel (goodness knows how he got hold of them). Proof, if you ask me, of what I have long suspected. That he has been up to mischief.'

'You think it was him that Chapman saw?'

'Yes I do, if he saw anything. His nerves were shot; so perhaps he saw what he expected to see. And now we have pretty good proof of who has been behind these break-ins. Who Chapman must have seen that night that so un-hinged him. Perhaps even what he saw the night he died: for having failed to find the mirror in the treasury, would it not be natural for Schwarzgruber or his proxies to search for it in Chapman's rooms in Pandy? Or even in my lodgings? I think that solves our little mystery, don't you? It seems as I suspected that our hospitality has been betrayed. I spoke to the senior tutors this morning and they agreed. I have confronted Schwarzgruber and told him he has to go. I shall be glad to see the back of him. I always thought the reasons for his visit may be more political than academic. Thanks to you we have flushed him out, and perhaps given them something to think about. So you see: we need fear nothing.'

On hearing this news I allowed myself to feel somewhat reassured. Fisher remained evasive, but he had spoken sense, and I was slightly ashamed of myself for falling victim to Chapman's fears. Either way, I was not about to stay in the college a moment longer than I had to.

We came up at last out of the cellar, and I went one more time to 'Pandy' to pack up my things. There were several books that would have to be returned to the library. As I was walking back there I had a curious sort of turn, when I could not remember where I was or what I was about. I staggered a little, and nearly fell, but after a while it passed. Perhaps it was relief.

It was in the library that I came upon Schwarzgruber. He was also packing up his papers and books. They were strewn across a large table, at which he had clearly been nesting for weeks. I must have been greatly on edge, for as I passed him I saw runic lettering amongst his notes, and I fairly recoiled with horror. A foolish fancy came into my head that he might have somehow cast some runes on me. How embarrassed I am of that. He must have seen my expression for he immediately reassured me:

'There is nothing sinister in these letters, Herr James. 'SS' is merely the abbreviated name of a political organisation in Germany, to which unfortunately my excavation team on the Thule project has to report. Politics gets in everywhere these days does it not?'

'Yes of course, forgive me,' I said, and moved on to the main desk to return my own books. But as I did so I felt the seed of an idea being planted in my head. I even felt a sudden lurch of hope. For had I not come across such a mechanism several times before? I believe it first cropped up in Hortolanus's commentary on the Tabula Smaragdina. It was just the sort of manoeuvre that appealed to the early-modern hermeticist.

The price of a soul, it said, could be paid by proxy. If certain words had power then they could be given to and read by another (whether innocent or self-sacrificing). By this means the magus could call and bend a demoniacal force to his will, without at the same time risking his own body and soul to the bargain. He had merely to slip the fatal words to another to read (or make another read them by force or some other trickery). He could thereby unlock all the demon's power whilst avoiding the lethal price to be paid for it, by passing on that horrid fate to another. Indeed this mechanism had achieved a sort of notoriety, as it was supposedly employed by the worst necromancers in order to dispose of their enemies. But there was no reason at all to think that the good could not use the same means to protect themselves from evil.

It was surely this that was described in the missing pages of the Liber Sextus – for had not Woodward called it something awful and un-Christian? It is hard to think of what else they could possibly have gone on to say. The more I think about it, the clearer I am that that is what they must have said.

If Fisher was right then Schwarzgruber was a despicable man. A man who clearly wished to acquire the show-stone. Acquire it by whatever means possible, and for whatever satanic purpose. He was a fanatic and a thief – perhaps even the killer (whether witting or not) of Chapman. There was no knowing what other evil acts he might commit, or what he intended to do if he got hold of it.

And, after all, if Fisher was right that Schwartzgrube's nefarious activities were all there was to this affair, then there could be no harm in what I determined now to do. If on the other hand there was any chance that Fisher was wrong, and that these events could not be rationalised away, then what else could save me now from Chapman's fate? It was almost certainly harmless nonsense, of course – but what if it was not?

Now if I could somehow slip the 'words of power' to Schwarzgruber, then I could perhaps deflect onto him whatever end now threatened me. And I could do it without danger to anyone else who came across them (since they would hardly be likely to be able to read Enochian). There was else nothing for it. I resolved on a desperate attempt.

Scurrying back to Pandy as fast as my old legs would go, I heaved breathlessly up the stairs. I seized the page on which I had written out the translation. If Schwarzgruber was so eager to know the secrets of the show-stone, then let him have them. I would find a way of giving him what I myself had wished I'd never read. If I could only get to him before he had finished packing his things, then perhaps I could somehow slip it amongst his papers and be free of it.

I had got halfway down the stairs again before I realised that would not do. For, with the full translation, Schwarzgruber might guess as I had done about the fatal Enochian wording, and pass it on to any innocent, and so the curse would spread. I could not in all conscience be the instrument of that – not if there was any truth in it. Better to shear off the other lines, and leave him totally in the dark. For, without the context, and knowing nothing of the book they were taken from, I could not see how he could conceivably know what these meaningless letters might entail, or that he could protect himself from them by passing them on as I had.

I staggered back up the stairs to Chapman's room. Hurriedly, I re-wrote on a single sheet the seven Enochian letters. Could they work in isolation? I could not see why not. Dee's book was clear that it was those seven syllables that unlocked the show-stone's power. Indeed I will destroy the original, so that no further copies of those evil syllables can ever be made again. Then this thing can be put safely away forever.

Finally I had it down:

161

I folded the note twice in half and tucked it at the back of a book of blank paper. I might easily put that down and – picking up the booklet alone – leave the sheet by a fortuitous 'accident' in the midst of his effects. Or, if I could only somehow distract the man's attention, I might be able to slip it unnoticed into his bag. After all, there was no stipulation about it having to be willingly accepted. By the time he had found and read it, he might be halfway back to Württemberg.

The journey back across the lawns to the library was very dreadful indeed. Shooting pains were running up and down the muscles in my legs. I am now too old to run, and can manage at best a sort of laboured trot. I felt a sudden dizziness, and a total loss of balance, so that I could hardly walk.

As I mounted the stairs to the library I felt sick to the stomach. I was panting for breath when I pushed open the double doors. He was gone!

The librarian noticed me enter and, baffled by my haste, came up and said:

'I'm sorry, Sir, if you're looking for that foreign gentleman, you've just missed him.'

Panicking, I rushed past him back into the quad. If he had left the College then I should never catch him. I forced myself to think. He had not had his baggage with him, so he must have returned to his guest room to pick that up. The porter told me in which room he had been staying. It was the far staircase in the Garden Quad. I was hobbling now by the time I reached it. Schwarzgruber's guest room was on the first floor. At last I was at his doors, which were ajar. I pushed in.

Schwarzgruber stood on the other side of the room, bent over his bed. As I entered he straightened up and looked at me.

'Herr James?!' he said, surprised. He had already closed up his suitcases, which stood by the door. On the bed was a travel bag, into which he was pushing the last of the things he had cleared from the library.

How to distract him for long enough to drop my paper into this bag? I tried to think of something to say to excuse my sudden visit. I blurted out the first thing that came into my head, and asked him why he was leaving us.

'I am forced to leave,' he said. 'There has been an interesting development at the dig in Gotland.'

He told the lie coolly, knowing I knew the real reason. He was standing full square between me and the open bag.

'That is a great pity!' I said, 'There was so much we could have discussed . . .'

My mind seized up as I tried to think of something – anything – to say to him next, let alone some way of distracting him for a moment. There was an awkward silence, broken only by my panting breath.

'Forgive me, Sir – my legs – I have over-exerted myself.'

'Excuse me. Please. Let me get for you a glass of water.'

He came and took my arm and led me into the room. He sat me down on the edge of the bed. This would be wonderfully easy after all. He turned from me and walked to the corner of the room, where there was a little washbasin. There was a mirror above it, though, in which he watched me as he turned on the tap. He overturned the little glass that stood on a shelf above the basin. His bag was on the other end of the bed. There was no way I could reach it without him seeing me get up. Between us, though, was a pile of his books. As he looked down for a second to fill the glass with water I lent across and put the folded sheet on top of them. Just then he turned back to the room and brought over the glass.

'I am so sorry, Professor-Doctor, I am making a fool of myself. And I am interrupting your packing. Thank you for this, I am better now. Let us shake hands and say goodbye.'

I could see he was slightly suspicious now, though he could not work out why I had come.

I was out of the door as fast as I could be whilst giving the appearance of being unhurried. I was on the first half-landing down when I heard, with mounting panic, Schwarzgruber open the door again above me.

'Herr James,' he called, 'you have forgotten something.'

His voice was soft but insistent. He stepped out onto the stairs with the paper in his outstretched hand. Here was the crisis. I put all on one last throw.

'Oh – I am a fool! – I quite forgot. I meant to give this to you, Professor-Doctor. It relates to the show-stone we were speaking of, and how it was used. I can't make head nor tail of it myself. I wondered if you might look at it. I thought after our talk the other night that it might be of some interest.'

Schwarzgruber stared at me incredulously. His suspicions soon gave way to an expression of un-looked-for and contemptuous triumph, which he barely tried to conceal.

'How kind, of you, Herr James.'

'Don't mention it, old thing,' I said, and turned again down the stairs. Schwarzgruber, in his eagerness to read it, did not wait for me to be out of sight, but strode back up to his room. I went down the rest of stairs as fast as I could go. He would be after me in moments, I knew, and there might be the Devil to pay if he caught me. No time to get across the College to the safety of the lodge before he did. Indeed, I would never make it across the quad and out of sight in either direction, before he should reach the door and see where I was going. There was no way now I could explain my actions or avoid taking back the note. Such an encounter would at best be embarrassing: at worst it might have dreadful results.

I was at ground level by now. With a sudden inspiration – instead of going outside – I continued down the stairs the final half-flight to the basement. I was already at the bottom when I heard him erupting out of his room and come charging down the stairs over my head. I should be cornered here if he chose to follow me down. But as I had prayed he went straight out and into the quad. Finding he could not see me, he ran off immediately towards the lodge. He no doubt hoped to catch me before I got to it, and to demand to know what I was about. From there it was a simple matter of following him out, watching him disappear into Great Quad, and then turning and hurrying away in the other direction. Once I had let myself out through the back of the College I knew that I was safe.

I immediately walked round to Simmons's house. I hoped to seek sanctuary there for an hour until the coast was clear. Nonsense or not, I was free of it. By now I was experiencing great waves of nausea and relief. The exertion, of course, and the sudden release of my fears, rendered me almost tearful with exhilaration. I can only suppose it was this that made me suddenly wish to unburden myself.

Simmons was at home and welcomed me in. His wife is much worse than when I last saw her. When I went through she screeched and babbled in a most unpleasant way, like a sort of grotesque glossolalia. Simmons was all apologies. He said he had only seen her like this once before, and suggested we take tea instead in his kitchen.

The man must be a saint to keep nursing her himself. It would, I think, be enough to challenge any man's faith. It was almost an insult to confide in him my own troubles. I also saw, with a mixed feeling of reproach and admiration, that his rather unorthodox mode of entertaining was deliberate policy. It was a refusal to be ashamed; and a challenge to the rest of the World not to take their own problems too seriously.

I am not used to discussing personal matters. It does not come easily to me. But the Reverend is a man I feel I can talk to about my burdens. He is such a sound fellow.

I told him I thought my intellectual powers were at an end – that there would be no more writing. I explained I had begun to question my actions in the War. And I asked him if it was wrong to put a bad man in the way of possible harm, if that was the only chance to prevent something worse.

The Reverend answered that he fears good men must sometimes confront evil with dark means. He added I was only doing my duty as I saw it, as Provost of one of the great institutions of the Empire. I could not have foreseen how terrible the War would be – none of us could. And even if we had not with all our zeal exhorted the boys to make their country proud, they still would have been called up in any case. I loved the boys so strongly. *I did my duty*.

I mentioned my other matter briefly, though I find I do not like to speak of it, especially to one who is not a fellow *Platonist*. I said I was afraid there might be something unspeakable in my mind. Something that I could not acknowledge to anyone – even myself. Of course I expected to be judged for what I have been and for what I have done. That it does not – it surely cannot – end here.

But what if it does, and this is all there is? Or what if the Dead don't go to a better place, but stay here among us? I challenged him openly on this score. I said I did not mind admitting I was afraid. I had seen Death on several occasions and could find no peace or hope in it.

Simmons smiled and gave his chins a thoughtful stroke, and said:

'Reason and Faith always banish superstitious night-mares in the end. And in any case, are you quite sure you are frightened of the *right things*? Death, for instance, is a curious thing to be scared of. For even if there isn't a blissful afterlife, you won't know anything about it. And as for the Dead, they surely cannot hurt us. It is not them we should be concerned about, but our own fears and desires. Faustian pacts are not made with sinister stran-gers, but with ourselves – when we allow ourselves to indulge our terrors and our instincts. Introspection with-out self-control may be dangerous, then, for it can reveal what it cannot contain. It is sometimes better not to look into these things in the first place.'

He added something consoling on how it is not our temptations and fears that define us, but how we face them. He told me to stay strong against fear *and* temptation, and said that the Church might help. He ended by saying we must have faith in the Goodness of the Almighty. Though he admits that the World now spins with so much cruelty and pain that even he himself sometimes has doubts of our Saviour. I was surprised at him and we said a prayer together.

But what if the things he had said before were right? That both the tenets of science and the consolations of Christianity are incompatible with the existence of demonic forces?

He answered with something very wise about real evil residing, not in haunted houses, but in thoughts in the minds of men. Men who acquire power, or spread evil ideas, and perhaps even tell themselves they are doing good. I shall try to remember that.

As for my recent actions: if he is right that my fears were misplaced then it follows I have done nothing wrong. In any case I can now feel myself swimming up again into the light, now that I have rid myself of curse and show-stone.

Fisher was bitterly disappointed when I told him I was leaving. I cited a previous engagement of long standing. But I was able to give him the show-stone, with a good description of its provenance, which after all was all I had been asked to do. I said I could tell him nothing else about it, and strongly advised him to leave it well alone. If he expected any more he should have been straight with me from the start. Or better still never got me involved in this wretched affair in the first place.

Then I burned Chapman's notes, and all mention of the Enochian letters, and everything else that referred to them. Finally I destroyed Dee's book, which was a terrible thing to do, but someone should have done it a long time ago. It offends all my instincts to set fire to a book. But it could be vital that no other copies of those awful words are ever made or read. I was sure by now that Schwarzgruber would have read the note, and be fine, and that these precautions of mine were completely unnecessary. But where the stakes are so high it is surely right to play it safe. The thing burned quickly, and was gone in an instant, leaving nothing but the charred remains of its binding, smoking in the grate.

Evening

Such a weight is lifted. I left on the afternoon train, albeit my leave-taking was awkward. And now I am away from the thing for good, and I feel a decade younger. Re-reading my journal, I am struck by what a toll the last few days have taken, and of how unwell I have been.

It is a great relief to arrive back at Eton. It is warmer here than at Oxford. The early winter we were promised has for the moment retreated. We are back to a muzzy late-autumnal dampness, with a mulch of rotting leaves underfoot. I am pretty much the sole inhabitant now that term is over. It is perhaps at such times that the School is fullest of memories: that I can recall most clearly the figures from when first I came, and of course those who are no longer with us. But I shall not allow myself to indulge in melancholic musings. I have had a scare, that is all, and it is over. I believe a bath, a tea, and a pipe will quite restore me to myself again. In all, however, I feel even more that a great weight has been lifted. It is such a relief to be safely back at home, and to find myself in my own cheerful rooms once more. I think that tonight I shall at last sleep soundly.

December 5th

Morning

I believe I slept quite peacefully until it happened.

Then suddenly I am dreaming. I am doing the rounds after prep and saying good night to the boys. I must traverse dark halls and empty chambers. There are foul thoughts in my head but I push them aside. I think I hear laughter from the stairs to the upper floor chambers. Presuming some of the boys are up and after some mischief, I follow the sound down the corridor to the old room on the North side.

I see some boys laughing provocatively and running in there to hide. I think I know before I go round that corner they are from my first third form, and that they are trying to lure me after them, but God forgive me I cannot help but follow. My mind is pleading not to go in but my legs propel me after them. Do I think perhaps I can save them? I enter the room and there they stand naked before me at last. Silent. Unnatural perversions. They are as they had been at that tender age, but – dear Christ! – also *not* as they had been. I will not blaspheme their memories by recording how they look. I shall only say it seems that I perjured myself. Perjured myself when I told the School in College Chapel they had died in an instant and had not suffered. I shall never forget how reproachfully they stare at me – dead faces with living eyes – as though it were I, and not the weapons of the enemy, that did those terrible things to their bodies. Then as one they raise a malicious laugh, and at last here they come reaching out towards me –

I fall and wake up and I am on my bed. But the mirror is on my bedside table, screaming, and I raise my head to look into it. In its reflection I see the window is open – black bars against green sky. And turning there is little Fanshawe. Such a fine child he had been, I remember him so lithe and pretty when I comforted him in the sick room. Now he is crawling lasciviously up my sheets. I cannot move. Oh Christ! – he is on top of me. I do not wake up. I cannot wake up. He drags himself up on my chest and pushes his cold face into mine. His mottled purple lips are upon my lips. His tongue is in my mouth. The slime from his lungs is in my throat. I finally half-manage to scream.

At last I am really awake, fighting for breath. I see Dr Burrows leaning over me and hear him tell me the news. It was an apoplexy, probably building for days. I try to speak to him but I can only mumble. The right side of my face is paralysed, what strength I have is faint. I cannot get out of bed. I am lying in my own filth. I lie like this for hours and I am utterly exhausted and sick, but I dare not go back to sleep.

Later, when they have cleaned me and I can sit up and write a little, I am able to over-hear Burrows talking to Matron. He believes that nervous stress has completely undone my health. There is talk of isolating me. He suggests I retire immediately for the good of the School. I must do my duty. I suppose I shall be confined to bed. The thought is too horrible to bear. *I know now that I shall never be free of them.*'

'And that, it seems, was the last decipherable entry in the journal of M R James. Attached to these re-discovered documents are some notes by Dr Burrows. They make clear he had a series of strokes over the next few weeks. These left him entirely bed-ridden as he made a final descent into vivid dementia. He never recovered, and died a few months later in his rooms at Eton. The Times obituary reported that he died peacefully in his bed. In bed is correct. But the rest of Burrow's notes suggest that peacefully is hardly the word.

Elsewhere Fishers' papers refer to a secret circle of German scholars, that called themselves the 'Sons of Alberich'. Fisher believed they were a division of the Ahnenerbe, a pseudo-archaeological body that was controlled by the SS. Schwarzgruber may have been a member, but his subsequent fate is unknown. Fisher found little enough evidence, but thought his visit was officially sanctioned: an attempt to acquire or destroy some powerful object in British hands.

The scrying mirror of Dr Dee remains at Old College, Oxford, where it has resided since the seventeenth century, and where it is still kept to this day. I can confirm that the College authorities will allow no access to it at all.

If James was concerned about the dangers of reading or copying Dee's Enochian letters without passing them on, he was remarkably foolish to write them up again the last time he set down his journal.

It seems Fisher removed all these pages from James's effects at Eton. They were placed in the Old College archives, after Fisher's own bizarre death in the spring of 1940. They have remained there unread ever since.

If you knew what I have suffered since I found them there, you would understand why I had to publish. But now of course you have read them too. It is no small thing to abuse your readers' trust.

But perhaps you will soon see what drove me to it.'

Historical Note

'If I am not careful,
something of this kind may happen to me.'
                                                            M R James

The author of this article may have been morally unreliable – as well as impugning the characters of two guiltless
men – but most of his factual details are hard to fault.

Montague Rhodes James was indeed Provost of Britain's
most famous public school until just before his death in
1936. He had previously worked both there and at Kings
College, Cambridge, successfully juggling his duties with
his scholarship and his writing. In life James was almost
pathologically repressed. This informed his natural reticence, which may be the secret of how he came to be Britain's greatest writer of ghost stories. His final decline, I
am pleased to say, was supposed to be more peaceful than
is made out here. In fact Lytton Strachey said of him that
had led 'a life without a jolt'.

   Nor is there any other proof that he was ever tortured
by guilt. He urged 'all the students who are capable
of doing so to serve their country' in the First World
War. Indeed he wrote the wording sent to the relatives
of those who died. Yet it is striking, even in his private
journals, how little emotional reaction he showed to their
slaughter.

In his personal life he was a confirmed bachelor. He had apparently chaste relationships with James McBride – who died after a botched appendix operation urged on him by James – and also with favourites amongst his pupils. It seems these involved no more than plying thirteen year old boys with port and letting them stay late in his lodge, talking about ghosts. Anthony Powell, who was a pupil when James was Provost, said that these 'love affairs were fascinating to watch'. Although he was fond of boys, though, there is no evidence that these – or any of his relationships – were ever physical, either in his own mind or in practice. They were probably no more than rather intense attachments: Platonic in the usual sense of the word.

It is interesting to note that about this time James interviewed the young Christopher Lee. Lee, amongst his many famous roles, was later to play James on screen. He cannot have made a good impression on him, since he was not admitted to the school.

As for ghosts, James always said he was an agnostic on the subject. Towards the end of his life, however, he claimed that he had as a boy seen a mad and malicious face – which he took to be supernatural – staring at him through the gate of his childhood home at Great Livermere. His final recorded comment on the subject as he lay dying was this: 'yes – we know there are such things – but we do not know the rules'.

Herbert Fisher, Statesman and Historian, was indeed Warden of his College, a post that he had taken over from William Spooner. He held it until his death in a freak accident in 1940, at about the time of the evacuations from Dunkirk. The War service hinted at above would not have been his only gift to national security. For after his death, somewhat surprisingly, his underpants were deployed in Operation Mincemeat.

The Ahnenerbe certainly existed. Amongst other things it searched for archaeological proof of advanced Germanic culture in the Dark Ages. These doomed investigations were commissioned by the SS, whose famous runic lettering we have seen shocking James. Himmler's bizarre racial theories and sinister occult beliefs, as described above by Fisher, are well known.

The description of Dr Dee (1527–1608) given by Simmons and the others is largely accurate. He was a man whose great learning in science and navigation was eclipsed by his bizarre submersion in magic and hermeticism. Indeed, this led to him being largely forgotten until James helped rehabilitate his reputation. Apart from the passage in Enochian, the quotes from Dee are all confirmed somewhere else in his writings, which James himself had catalogued (there is no surviving 'Sixth Book of Mystery', though such 'mirror books' were common at the time). They remain a vivid, visionary, and highly disturbing enigma.

As for Dee's mirror, there are no other records of it. But a similar example of similar provenance exists. It was used by Dee in exactly the manner described. It was later owned by Horace Walpole, the antiquarian and father of English supernatural fiction. Walpole called it 'The Devile's Looking-Glasse'. It can be seen to this day in the British Museum. It throws a horrid reflection.

Michael Woodward was Warden of the same college at the time of the Great Plague. John Quinbey was certainly real, and really was locked in the Bell Tower until he died of starvation. However, the college records suggest it was not Woodward who was at fault but a predecessor – and that he had condemned Quinbey for blasphemy and heresy, rather than alchemy and witchcraft.

Both Woodward and Quinbey seem to have been exposing themselves to dangerous levels of mercury. Mercury toxaemia, common at a time when many medicines were made of it, induces symptoms of extreme paranoia, hallucination, and madness.

At this time the first discovery of another element was being made: phosphorus. It was extracted from human urine by the alchemist Hennig Brand, who was looking for the Philosopher's stone.

Quinbey, as he appears in this article, seems to display Idiot Savantic behaviour, similar to that of his contemporary, Isaac Newton. It was in 1665-6, when Newton was able to flee a plague-ridden Cambridge, that he made his great breakthroughs in Calculus, Gravitation, and Optics. He once almost blinded himself by putting a needle 'betwixt (his) eye and the bone, as near to the backside of the eye as (he) could'.

The other macabre optical experiments attributed here to Quinbey are similar to those of the Seventeenth Century philosopher René Descartes. He also owes to Descartes the metaphor of the 'Malicious Demon', who renders the evidence of both our Reason and our senses unreliable.

Descartes famously argued, as have many since, that it is possible to know whether or not you are dreaming. I believe he is wrong. I do not know whether he, James, or Woodward ever suffered from hypnopompic hallucination – that unhappy compound of sleep paralysis and lucid dreaming, that gives rise in so many cultures to the myth of the succubus or incubus. I have, and I cannot recommend it.

We know the Invisible College really existed, but it is usually reported to have numbered only twelve. Its members included Christopher Wren, Robert Boyle, and Robert Hooke. They met in Oxford to conduct experiments and observations, including of the Comet of Christmas 1664. Wren performed an experimental removal of the spleen of a living dog, which survived the procedure unharmed. This was at a time when human dissection by non-doctors was illegal. The results of their more minute observations – which included the first living cells ever seen – were published by Hooke in 1665 as a book called the 'Micrographia'. It caused a major sensation, not least for its famous diagram of a magnified flea.

It was unknown at the time that the Bubonic Plague, which last erupted in Britain in the same year, was borne by fleas. The policy of killing all cats and dogs, which might have kept down the number of flea-bearing rats, is thought to have contributed to the disaster. It is estimated that the disease killed 100,000 in London alone, and some densely populated areas experienced 75% mortality.

The story told by Jenkins to the Warden is also part of real college folklore. It matches almost word for word a true story told to me by a night porter at the same college; a man who I should add was neither credulous nor foolish nor drunk.

The inscription which is described above as being attached to the mirror turns out to be in dog Latin, simply encrypted. It is somewhat surprising that James could not break the easy cipher, since he uses the same code in his story on the 'Treasure of Abbot Thomas'. It is fairly easy to decipher.

This can be done by skipping one letter, then two, then three, then repeating the process. So you take the first letter of the code, then the third, then the sixth, then the tenth in the sequence. Then you start the same procedure with the twelfth, the fifteenth, the nineteenth, and so on. Having removed these letters and spelt them out, you add the alternate remaining letters.

This gives you the following inscription, doubtless intended by Dee as some sort of warning, perhaps to frighten unsuitable people from using his divination equipment:

Cave qui acrius aspicis ne displiceat quod monstrem!

For what it is worth I have had it translated and it comes out as follows:

Beware! – you who look too closely lest you do not like what I show you.

Postscript: M R James vs Edgar Allan Poe

> *'There were much of the beautiful, much of the wanton,*
> *much of the bizarre, something of the terrible,*
> *and not a little of that which might have excited disgust.'*
>
> Edgar Allan Poe

One of the themes of this book is a debate – that dates back as far as Ann Radcliffe – about two styles of supernatural fiction. Those two styles are exemplified by the two greatest writers of the genre: M R James and Edgar Allen Poe. So, though painfully conscious of the unflattering contrast, I have included one each of their best stories.

A Warning to the Curious

Despite his cosy settings, James always produces 'a pleasing terror'. But what elevates his works to greatness is how much more there is going on in them than initially meets the eye. So, unlike most examples of the genre, they improve upon re-reading. Indeed on closer examination many of them are not really *ghost* stories at all, but tales of witchcraft and demonology, with worrying philosophical implications.

In his famous 'Oh Whistle and I'll Come to You, My Lad', for example, the thing that attacks Parkins is no classic Victorian winding-sheet ghost. Rather it is more likely a Baphometic demon, worshipped by the Knights Templar who are hinted to have made the whistle. The Templars were supressed for sodomy as well as devil-worship, and there is a strong subliminal suggestion of homosexual fear in this story (even the title alludes to a sexual proposition), as Parkins finds out 'who is this who is coming' to share his bedroom.

The same can be said of what is perhaps James's greatest story: 'A Warning to the Curious'. Repressed homosexual panic can again be detected – from the moment the revenant scrabbles onto Paxton's back, to the final monstrous embrace that awaits him on the shore.

And again, there is an interesting subtext. James seems to have invented the legend of the three crowns that guard the coast. He was probably inspired by the heraldic arms of the Saxon Kingdom of East Anglia. But it is certainly 'not inconsistent with the rules of folklore'. Indeed it works so well that it later became a real local myth.

Seaburgh is James's version of Aldeburgh – a small Suffolk resort that he visited on many occasions, not far from the (then unexcavated) barrow at Sutton Hoo. The village is noted for its large Martello tower – where the horrifying denouement takes place – and the settlement that once surrounded it but now is lost to the sea. What could be a more suitable location for a story about invasion anxiety than crumbling Napoleonic coastal defences? That the underlying theme of the story is not personal but national jeopardy was clearer in an original version. That draft explicitly dates the action to 1917, when fears of a Germanic incursion were all too real.

If there is a moral to any of James's stories it is spelled out by the title of this one. It reveals his ambivalence about his antiquarian pursuits. This seems less surprising when you realise these led him into academia – and away from following his father into a career in the church. The real terror in James is not just the nasties such researches throw up, but the challenge that they pose to the reassurance of religious orthodoxy.

In any case it is carelessness with the past, not mere curiosity about it, that is usually the cause of the trouble to his protagonists. Again this is unsurprising for a conservative like James. In 'A Warning to the Curious' cultural vandalism is a threat not just to the vandal, but indeed to the nation. For if the crown has supernatural protection, might it not also have the supernatural power with which its protectors credited it? Better to proceed cautiously, or to leave things as they are.

The Masque of the Red Death

Of all Poe's strange tales, 'The Masque of the Red Death' may be the strangest. Prince Prospero is a sophisticated if amoral Renaissance virtuoso. The claustrophobic setting in which he immures himself owes much to the frame story in Boccaccio's Decameron. But the seven coloured chambers in which the action takes place, with their dream-like quality and uncertain symbolism, are a touch of pure Poe.

By turns exquisite, hallucinatory, claustrophobic, and delirious, the story has all the vivid intensity of an intoxicated or opiatenightmare, and all the inevitability of the best dark fairy tale. But if it is a fairy tale then what is its moral? What makes it so memorable and disturbing is that it apparently does not have one. Except perhaps the danger of believing that 'the external World could take care of itself. In the meantime it was folly to grieve, or to think.'

Poe himself was no stranger to alcohol or opium (they are both possible explanations for his mysterious death: a suitably bizarre end which itself would make a good subject for a novel). Nor need we look far for the psychological sources of his stories. If James's fears centred around sex, faith, and change, then Poe's focused on guilt, premature burial, and morbid sexual obsession (he married a 13 year old cousin, who then died slowly in front of him, all the while blaming his infidelities as the cause of her demise). These themes come up again and again in his 'Tales of the Grotesque'.

But 'The Masque of the Red Death' is something of a departure from Poe's usual leitmotifs. Here the source of fear is disease. As he was writing it his young wife was dying of tuberculosis; an illness which had probably already killed his foster-mother, mother, and brother. We are no longer as frightened of infectious diseases as we were in the past, and as perhaps we still should be. But, with Poe as with James, it is the deeper sense of existential dread that overwhelms the reader.

Whether it is plague or war which threatens their characters, it is the way they mirror our metaphysical anxieties which make these stories of the supernatural so compelling.

Prospero's Mirror

This has parallels in real life, where we are often afraid of the wrong things, and where our own self-fulfilling fears themselves can prove to be our undoing. That is why a ghost story does not need to have a ghost; or rather, why its rational explanations can be more disturbing than its supernatural ones. Whether it is real ghosts or witch-craft which destroy the protagonists in Prospero's Mirror, or whether it is natural causes provoked by their own fears, or whether the fears are merely the form taken by a demonic force, it is those deep fears themselves that seem to be the source ofthe trouble.

An object or book which reflects such fears can symbolise how disconcerting – even how dangerous – it may be to glimpse hidden parts of ourselves if we cannot control them or change them. So it does not matter whether Prospero is Dr Dee or Warden Woodward or M R James, or whether his 'mirror' is after all a looking-glass or a book. The artefact would be powerless except that it shows us what is inside us. Ultimately it is not the problem – we are.

M R James – A Warning to the Curious

The place on the east coast which the reader is asked to consider is Seaburgh. It is not very different now from what I remember it to have been when I was a child. Marshes intersected by dykes to the south, recalling the early chapters of Great Expectations; flat fields to the north, merging into heath; heath, fir woods, and, above all, gorse, inland. A long sea-front and a street: behind that a spacious church of flint, with a broad, solid western tower and a peal of six bells. How well I remember their sound on a hot Sunday in August, as our party went slowly up the white, dusty slope of road towards them, for the church stands at the top of a short, steep incline. They rang with a flat clacking sort of sound on those hot days, but when the air was softer they were mellower too. The railway ran down to its little terminus farther along the same road. There was a gay white windmill just before you came to the station, and another down near the shingle at the south end the town, and yet others on higher ground to the north. There were cottages of bright red brick with slate roofs . . . but why do I encumber you with these commonplace details? The fact is that they come crowding to the point of the pencil when it begins to write of Seaburgh. I should like to be sure that I had allowed the right ones to get on to the paper. But I forgot. I have not quite done with the word-painting business yet.

Walk away from the sea and the town, pass the station, and turn up the road on the right. It is a sandy road, parallel with the railway, and if you follow it, it climbs to somewhat higher ground. On your left (you are now going northward) is heath, on your right (the side towards the sea) is a belt of old firs, wind-beaten, thick at the top, with the slope that old seaside trees have; seen on the sky-line from the train they would tell you in an instant, if you did not know it, that you were approaching a windy coast. Well, at the top of my little hill, a line of these firs strikes out and runs towards the sea, for there is a ridge that goes that way; and the ridge ends in a rather well-defined mound commanding the level fields of rough grass, and a little knot of fir trees crowns it. And here you may sit on a hot spring day, very well content to look at blue sea, white windmills, red cottages bright green grass, church tower, and distant martello tower on the south.

As I have said, I began to know Seaburgh as a child; but a gap of a good many years separates my early knowledge from that which is more recent. Still it keeps its place in my affections, and any tales of it that I pick up have an interest for me. One such tale is this: it came to me in a place very remote from Seaburgh, and quite accidentally, from a man whom 1 had been able to oblige – enough in his opinion to justify his making me his confidant to this extent.

I know all that country more or less (he said). I used to go to Seaburgh pretty regularly for golf in the spring. I generally put up at the 'Bear', with a friend – Henry Long it was, you knew him perhaps – ('Slightly,' I said) and we used to take a sitting-room and be very happy there. Since he died I haven't cared to go there. And I don't know that I should anyhow after the particular thing that happened on our last visit.

It was in April, 19–, we were there, and by some chance we were almost the only people in the hotel. So the ordinary public rooms were practically empty, and we were the more surprised when, after dinner, our sitting-room door opened, and a young man put his head in. We were aware of this young man. He was rather a rabbity anaemic subject – light hair and light eyes – but not unpleasing. So when he said: 'I beg your pardon, is this a private room?' we did not growl and say: 'Yes, it is,' but Long said, or I did – no matter which: 'Please come in.' 'Oh, may I?' he said, and seemed relieved. Of course it was obvious that he wanted company; and as he was a reasonable kind of person – not the sort to bestow his whole family history on you – we urged him to make himself at home. 'I dare say you find the other rooms rather bleak,' I said. Yes, he did: but it was really too good of us, and so on. That being got over, he made some pretence of reading a book.Long was playing Patience, I was writing. It became plain to me after a few minutes that this visitor of ours was in rather a state of fidgets or nerves, which communicated itself to me, and so I put away my writing and turned to at engaging him in talk.

After some remarks, which I forget, he became rather confidential. 'You'll think it very odd of me' (this was the sort of way he began), 'but the fact is I've had something of a shock.' Well, I recommended a drink of some cheering kind, and we had it. The waiter coming in made an interruption (and I thought our young man seemed very jumpy when the door opened), but after a while he got back to his woes again. There was nobody he knew in the place, and he did happen to know who we both were (it turned out there was some common acquaintance in town), and really he did want a word of advice, if we didn't mind. Of course we both said: 'By all means,' or 'Not at all,' and Long put away his cards. And we settled down to hear what his difficulty was.

'It began,' he said, 'more than a week ago, when I bicycled over to Froston, only about five or six miles, to see the church; I'm very much interested in architecture, and it's got one of those pretty porches with niches and shields. I took a photograph of it, and then an old man who was tidying up in the churchyard came and asked if I'd care to look into the church. I said yes, and he produced a key and let me in. There wasn't much inside, but I told him it was a nice little church, and he kept it very clean, "But," I said, "the porch is the best part of it." We were just outside the porch then, and he said, "Ah, yes, that is a nice porch; and do you know, sir, what's the meanin' of that coat of arms there?"

'It was the one with the three crowns, and though. I'm not much of a herald, I was able to say yes, I thought it was the old arms of the kingdom of East Anglia.

'"That's right, sir," he said, "and do you know the meanin' of them three crowns that's on it?"

'I said I'd no doubt it was known, but I couldn't recollect to have heard it myself.

'"Well, then," he said, "for all you're a scholard, I can tell you something you don't know. Them's the three 'oly crowns what was buried in the ground near by the coast to keep the Germans from landing – ah, I can see you don't believe that. But I tell you, if it hadn't have been for one of them 'oly crowns bein' there still, them Germans

192

would a landed here time and again, they would. Landed with their ships, and killed man, woman and child in their beds. Now then, that's the truth what I'm telling you, that is; and if you don't believe me, you ast the rector. There he comes: you ast him, I says."

'I looked round, and there was the rector, a nice-looking old man, coming up the path; and before I could begin assuring my old man, who was getting quite excited, that I didn't disbelieve him, the rector struck in, and said:

"What's all this about, John? Good day to you, sir. Have you been looking at our little church?"'

'So then there was a little talk which allowed the old man to calm down, and then the rector asked him again what was the matter.

"Oh," he said, "it warn't no think, only I was telling this gentleman he'd ought to ast you about them 'oly crowns."

"Ah, yes, to be sure," said the rector, "that's a very curious matter, isn't it? But I don't know whether the gentleman is interested in our old stories, eh?"

"Oh, he'll be interested fast enough," says the old man, "he'll put his confidence in what you tells him, sir; why, you known William Ager yourself, father and son too."

'Then I put in a word to say how much I should like to hear all about it, and before many minutes I was walking up the village street with the rector, who had one or two words to say to parishioners, and then to the rectory, where he took me into his study. He had made out, on the way, that I really was capable of taking an intelligent interest in a piece of folklore, and not quite the ordinary tripper. So he was very willing to talk, and it is rather surprising to me that the particular legend he told me has not made its way into print before. His account of it was this: "There has always been a belief in these parts in the three holy crowns. The old people say they were buried in different places near the coast to keep off the Danes or the French or the Germans. And they say that one of the three was dug up a long time ago, and another has disappeared by the encroaching of the sea, and one's still left doing its work, keeping off invaders. Well, now, if you have read the ordinary guides and histories of this county, you will remember perhaps that in 1687 a crown, which was said to be the crown of Redwald, King of the East Angles, was dug up at Rendlesham, and alas! alas! melted down before it was even properly described or drawn. Well, Rendlesham isn't on the coast, but it isn't so very far inland, and it's on a very important line of access. And I believe that is the crown which the people mean when they say that one has been dug up. Then on the south you don't want me to tell you where there was a Saxon royal palace which is now under the sea, eh? Well, there was the second crown, I take it. And up beyond these two, they say, lies the third."

"'Do they say where it is?'" of course I asked.

'He said, "Yes, indeed, they do, but they don't tell," and his manner did not encourage me to put the obvious question. Instead of that I waited a moment, and said: "What did the old man mean when he said you knew William Ager, as if that had something to do with the crowns?"

"'To be sure," he said, "now that's another curious story. These Agers it's a very old name in these parts, but I can't find that they were ever people of quality or big owners these Agers say, or said, that their branch of the family were the guardians of the last crown. A certain old Nathaniel Ager was the first one I knew – I was born and brought up quite near here – and he, I believe, camped out at the place during the whole of the war of 1870. William, his son, did the same, I know, during the South African War. And young William, his son, who has only died fairly recently, took lodgings at the cottage nearest the spot; and I've no doubt hastened his end, for he was a consumptive, by exposure and night watching. And he was the last of that branch. It was a dreadful grief to him to think that he was the last, but he could do nothing, the only relations at all near to him were in the colonies. I wrote letters for him to them imploring them to come over on business very important to the family, but there has been no answer. So the last of the holy crowns, if it's there, has no guardian now."

'That was what the rector told me, and you can fancy how interesting I found it. The only thing I could think of when I left him was how to hit upon the spot where the crown was supposed to be. I wish I'd left it alone.

'But there was a sort of fate in it, for as I bicycled back past the churchyard wall my eye caught a fairly new grave-stone, and on it was the name of William Ager. Of course I got off and read it. It said "of this parish, died at Seaburgh, 19– , aged 28." There it was, you see. A little judicious questioning in the right place, and I should at least find the cottage nearest the spot. Only I didn't quite know what was the right place to begin my questioning at. Again there was fate: it took me to the curiosity-shop down that way – you know – and I turned over some old books, and, if you please, one was a prayer-book of 1740 odd, in a rather handsome binding – I'll just go and get it, it's in my room.'

He left us in a state of some surprise, but we had hardly time to exchange any remarks when he was back, panting, and handed us the book opened at the fly-leaf, on which was, in a straggly hand:

'Nathaniel Ager is my name and England is my nation,

Seaburgh is my dwelling-place and Christ is my Salvation,

When I am dead and in my Grave, and all my bones are rotton,

I hope the lord will think on me when I am quite forgotton.'

This poem was dated 1754, and there were many more entries of Agers, Nathaniel, Frederick, William, and so on, ending with William, 19– .

'You see,' he said, 'anybody would call it the greatest bit of luck. I did, but I don't now. Of course I asked the shopman about William Ager, and of course he happened to remember that he lodged in a cottage in the North Field and died there. This was just chalking the road for me. I knew which the cottage must be: there is only one sizable one about there. The next thing was to scrape some sort of acquaintance with the people, and I took a walk that way at once. A dog did the business for me: he made at me so fiercely that they had to run out and beat him off, and then naturally begged my pardon, and we got into talk. I had only to bring up Ager's name, and pretend I knew, or thought I knew something of him, and then the woman said how sad it was him dying so young, and she was sure it came of him spending the night out of doors in the cold weather. Then I had to say: "Did he go out on the sea at night?" and she said: "Oh, no, it was on the hillock yonder with the trees on it." And there I was.

'I know something about digging in these barrows: I've opened many of them in the down country. But that was with owner's leave, and in broad daylight and with men to help. I had to prospect very carefully here before

I put a spade in: I couldn't trench across the mound, and with those old firs growing there I knew there would be awkward tree loots. Still the soil was very light and sandy and easy, and there was a rabbit hole or so that might be developed into a sort of tunnel. The going out and coming back at odd hours to the hotel was going to be the awkward part. When I made up my mind about the way to excavate I told the people that I was called away for a night, and I spent it out there. I made my tunnel: I won't bore you with the details of how I supported it and filled it in when I'd done, but the main thing is that I got the crown.'

Naturally we both broke out into exclamations of surprise and interest. I for one had long known about the finding of the crown at Rendlesham and had often lamented its fate. No one has ever seen an Anglo-Saxon crown – at least no one had. But our man gazed at us with a rueful eye. 'Yes,' he said, 'and the worst of it is I don't know how to put it back.'

'Put it back?' we cried out. 'Why, my dear sir, you've made one of the most exciting finds ever heard of in this country. Of course it ought to go to the Jewel House at the Tower. What's your difficulty? If you're thinking about the owner of the land, and treasure-trove, and all that, we can certainly help you through. Nobody's going to make a fuss about technicalities in a case of this kind.'

Probably more was said, but all he did was to put his face in his hands, and mutter: 'I don't know how to put it back.'

At last Long said: 'You'll forgive me, I hope, if I seem impertinent, but are you quite sure you've got it?' I was wanting to ask much the same question myself, for of course the story did seem a lunatic's dream when one thought over it. But I hadn't quite dared to say what might hurt the poor young man's feelings. However, he took it quite calmly – really, with the calm of despair, you might say. He sat up and said: 'Oh, yes, there's no doubt of that: I have it here, in my loom, locked up in my bag. You can come and look at it if you like: I won't offer to bring it here.'

We were not likely to let the chance slip. We went with him; his room was only a few doors off. The boots was just collecting shoes in the passage: or so we thought: afterwards we were not sure. Our visitor – his name was Parton – was in a worse state of shivers than before, and went hurriedly into the room, and beckoned us after him, turned on the light, and shut the door carefully. Then he unlocked his kit-bag, and produced a bundle of clean pocket-handkerchief in which something was wrapped, laid it on the bed, and undid it. I can now say I have seen an actual Anglo-Saxon crown. It was of silver – as the Rendlesham one is always said to have been – it was set with some gems, mostly antique intaglios and cameos, and was of rather plain, almost rough workmanship. In fact, it was like those you see on the coins and in the man-uscripts. I found no reason to think it was later than the ninth century. I was intensely interested, of course, and I wanted to turn it over in my hands, but Paxton prevented me. 'Don't you touch it,' he said, 'I'll do that.' And with a sigh that was, I declare to you, dreadful to hear, he took it up and turned it about so that we could see every part of it. 'Seen enough?' he said at last, and we nodded. He wrapped it up and locked it in his bag, and stood looking at us dumbly. 'Come back to our room,' Long said, 'and tell us what the trouble is.' He thanked us, and said: 'Will you go first and see if – if the coast is clear?' That wasn't very intelligible, for our proceedings hadn't been, after all, very suspicious, and the hotel, as I said, was practically empty. However, we were beginning to have inklings of – we didn't know what, and anyhow nerves are infectious. So we did go, first peering out as we opened the door, and fancying (I found we both had the fancy) that a shadow, or more than a shadow – but it made no sound – passed from before us to one side as we came out into the passage. 'It's all right,' we whispered to Paxton – whispering seemed the proper tone – and we went, with him between us, back to our sitting-room. I was preparing, when we got there, to be ecstatic about the unique interest of what we had seen, but when I looked at Paxton I saw that would be terribly out of place, and I left it to him to begin.

'What *is* to be done?' was his opening. Long thought it right (as he explained to me afterwards) to be obtuse, and said: 'Why not find out who the owner of the land is, and inform –' Oh, no, no!' Paxton broke in impatiently, 'I beg your pardon: you've been very kind, but don't you see it's got to go back, and I daren't be there at night, and daytime's impossible. Perhaps, though, you don't see: well, then, the truth is that I've never been alone since I touched it.' I was beginning some fairly stupid comment, but Long caught my eye, and I stopped. Long said: 'I think I do see, perhaps: but wouldn't it be a relief – to tell us a little more clearly what the situation is?'

Then it all came out: Paxton looked over his shoulder and beckoned to us to come nearer to him, and began speaking in a low voice: we listened most intently, of course, and compared notes afterwards, and I wrote down our version, so I am confident I have what he told us almost word for word. He said: 'It began when I was first prospecting, and put me off again and again. There was always somebody – a man – standing by one of the firs. This was in daylight, you know. He was never in front of me. I always saw him with the tail of my eye on the left or the right, and he was never there when I looked straight for him. I would lie down for quite a long time and take careful observations, and make sure there was no one, and then when I got up and began prospecting again, there he was. And he began to give me hints, besides; for wherever I put that prayer-book – short of locking it up, which I did at last – when I came back to my loom it was always out on my table open at the fly-leaf where the names are, and one of my razors across it to keep it open. I'm sure he just can't open my bag, or something more would have happened. You see, he's light and weak, but all the same I daren't face him. Well, then, when I was making the tunnel, of course it was worse, and if I hadn't been so keen I should have dropped the whole thing and run. It was like someone scraping at my back all the time: I thought for a long time it was only soil dropping on me, but as I got nearer the – the crown, it was unmistakable. And when I actually laid it bare and got my fingers into the ring of it and pulled it out, there came a sort of cry behind me – oh, I can't tell you how desolate it was! And horribly threatening too. It spoilt all my pleasure in my find – cut it off that moment. And if I hadn't been the wretched. fool I am, I should have put the thing back and left it. But I didn't. The rest of the time was just awful. I had hours to get through before I could decently come back to the hotel. First I spent time filling up my tunnel and covering my tracks, and all the while he was there trying to thwart me. Sometimes, you know, you see him, and sometimes you don't, just as he pleases,

I think: he's there, but he has some power over your eyes. Well, I wasn't off the spot very long before sunrise, and then I had to get to the junction for Seaburgh, and take a train back. And though it was daylight fairly soon, I don't know if that made it much better. There were always hedges, or gorse-bushes, or park fences along the road – some sort of cover, I mean – and I was never easy for a second. And then when I began to meet people going to work, they always looked behind me very strangely: it might have been that they were surprised at seeing anyone so early; but I didn't think it was only that, and I don't now: they didn't look exactly at me. And the porter at the train was like that too. And the guard held open the door after I'd got into the carriage – just as he would if there was somebody else coming, you know. Oh, you may be very sure it isn't my fancy,' he said with a dull sort of laugh. Then he went on: 'And even if I do get it put back, he won't forgive me: I can tell that. And I was so happy a fortnight ago.' He dropped into a chair, and I believe he began to cry.

We didn't know what to say, but we felt we must come to the rescue somehow, and so – it really seemed the only thing – we said if he was so set on putting the crown back in its place, we would help him. And I must say that after what we had heard it did seem the right thing. If these horrid consequences had come on this poor man, might there not really be something in the original idea of the crown having some curious power bound up with it, to guard the coast? At least, that was my feeling, and I think it was Long's too. Our offer was very welcome to Paxton, anyhow. When could we do it? It was nearing half-past ten. Could we contrive to make a late walk plausible to the hotel people that very night? We looked out of the window: there was a brilliant full moon – the Paschal moon. Long undertook to tackle the boots and propitiate him. He was to say that we should not be much over the hour, and if we did find it so pleasant that we stopped out a bit longer we would see that he didn't lose by sitting up. Well, we were pretty regular customers of the hotel, and did not give much trouble, and were considered by the servants to be not under the mark in the way of tips; and so the boots was propitiated, and let us out on to the sea-front, and remained, as we heard later, looking after us. Paxton had a large coat over his arm, under which was the wrapped-up crown.

So we were off on this strange errand before we had time to think how very much out of the way it was. I have told this part quite shortly on purpose, for it really does represent the haste with which we settled our plan and took action. 'The shortest way is up the hill and through the churchyard,' Paxton said, as we stood a moment before, the hotel looking up and down the front. There was nobody about – nobody at all. Seaburgh out of the season is an early, quiet place. 'We can't go along the dyke by the cottage, because of the dog,' Paxton also said, when I pointed to what I thought a shorter way along the front and across two fields. The reason he gave was good enough. We went up the road to the church, and turned in at the churchyard gate. I confess to having thought that there might be some lying there who might be conscious of our business: but if it was so, they were also conscious that one who was on their side, so to say, had us under surveillance, and we saw no sign of them. But under observation we felt we were, as I have never felt it at another time. Specially was it so when we passed out of the churchyard into a narrow path with close high hedges, through which we hurried as Christian did through that Valley; and so got out into open fields. Then along hedges, though I world sooner have been in the open, where I could see if anyone was visible behind me; over a gate or two, and then a swerve to the left, taking us up on to the ridge which ended in that mound.

As we neared it, Henry Long felt, and I felt too, that there were what I can only call dim presences waiting for us, as well as a far more actual one attending us. Of Paxton's agitation all this time I can give you no adequate picture: he breathed like a hunted beast, and we could not either of us look at his face. How he would manage when we got to the very place we had not troubled to think: he had seemed so sure that that would not be difficult. Nor was it. I never saw anything like the dash with which he flung himself at a particular spot in the side of the mound, and tore at it, so that in a very few minutes the greater part of his body was out of sight. We stood holding the coat and that bundle of handkerchief, and looking, very fearfully, I must admit, about us. There was nothing to be seen: a line of dark firs behind us made one skyline, more trees and the church tower half a mile off on the right, cottages and a windmill on the horizon on the left, calm sea dead in front, faint barking of a dog at a cottage on a gleaming dyke between us and it: full moon making that path we know across the sea: the eternal whisper of the Scotch firs just above us, and of the sea in front. Yet, in all this quiet, an acute, an acrid consciousness of a restrained hostility very near us, like a dog on a leash that might be let go at any moment.

Paxton pulled himself out of the hole, and stretched a hand back to us. 'Give it to me,' he whispered, 'unwrapped.' We pulled off the handkerchiefs, and he took the crown.

The moonlight just fell on it as he snatched it. We had not ourselves touched that bit of metal, and I have thought since that it was just as well. In another moment Paxton was out of the hole again and busy shovelling back the soil with hands that were already bleeding. He would have none of our help though It was much the longest part of the job to get the place to look undisturbed yet – I don't know how – he made a wonderful success of it. At last he was satisfied and we turned back.

We were a couple of hundred yards from the hill when Long suddenly said to him: 'I say you've left your coat there. That won't do. See?' And I certainly did see it – the long dark overcoat lying where the tunnel had been. Paxton had not stopped, however: he only shook his head, and held up the coat on his arm. And when we joined him, he said, without any excitement, but as if nothing mattered any more: 'That wasn't my coat.' And, indeed, when we looked back again, that dark thing was not to be seen.

Well, we got out on to the road, and came rapidly back that way. It was well before twelve when we got in, trying to put a good face on it, and saying – Long and I – what a lovely night it was for a walk. The boots was on the look-out for us, and we made remarks like that for his edification as we entered the hotel. He gave another look up and down the sea-front before he locked the front door, and said: 'You didn't meet many people about, I s'pose, sir?' 'No, indeed, not a soul,' I said; at which I remember Paxton looked oddly at me. 'Only I thought I see someone turn up the station road after you gentlemen,' said the boots. 'Still, you was three together, and I don't suppose he meant mischief.' I didn't know what to say; Long merely said 'Good night,' and we went off upstairs, promising to turn put all lights, and to go to bed in a few minutes.

Back in our room, we did our very best to make Paxton take a cheerful view. 'There's the crown safe back,' we said; 'very likely you'd have done better not to touch it' (and he heavily assented to that), 'but no real harm has been done, and we shall never give this away to anyone who would be so mad as to go near it. Besides, don't you feel better yourself? I don't mind confessing,' I said, 'that on the way there I was very much inclined to take your view about – well, about being followed; but going back, it wasn't at all the same thing, was it?' No, it wouldn't do: '*You've* nothing to trouble yourselves about,' he said, 'but I'm not forgiven. I've got to pay for that miserable sacrilege still. I know what you are going to say. The Church might help. Yes, but it's the body that has to suffer. It's true I'm not feeling that he's waiting outside for me just now. But –' Then he stopped. Then he turned to thanking us, and we put him off as soon as we could. And naturally we pressed him to use our sitting-room next day, and said we should be glad to go out with him. Or did he play golf, perhaps? Yes, he did, but he didn't think he should care about that tomorrow. Well, we recommended him to get up late and sit in our room in the morning while we were playing, and we would have a walk later in the day. He was very submissive and *piano* about it all: ready to do just what we thought best, but clearly quite certain in his own mind that what was coming could not be averted or palliated. You'll wonder why we didn't insist on accompanying him to his home and seeing him safe into the care of brothers or someone. The fact was he had nobody. He had had a flat in town, but lately he had made up his mind to settle for a time in Sweden, and he had dismantled his flat and shipped off his belongings, and was whiling away a fortnight or three weeks before he made a start. Anyhow, we didn't see what we could do better than sleep on it – or not sleep very much, as was my case and see what we felt like tomorrow morning.

We felt very different, Long and I, on as beautiful an April morning as you could desire; and Paxton also looked very different when we saw him at breakfast. 'The first approach to a decent night I seem ever to have had,' was what he said. But he was going to do as we had settled: stay in probably all the morning, and come out with us later. We went to the links; we met some other men and played with them in the morning, and had lunch there rather early, so as not to be late back. All the same, the snares of death overtook him.

Whether it could have been prevented, I don't know. I think he would have been got at somehow, do what we might. Anyhow, this is what happened.

We went straight up to our room. Paxton was there, reading quite peaceably. 'Ready to come out shortly?' said Long, 'say in half an hour's time?' 'Certainly,' he said: and I said we would change first, and perhaps have baths, and call for him in half an hour. I had my bath first, and went and lay down on my bed, and slept for about ten minutes. We came out of our rooms at the same time, and went together to the sitting-room. Paxton wasn't there – only his book. Nor was he in his room, nor in the downstair rooms. We shouted for him. A servant came out and said: 'Why, I thought you gentlemen was gone out already, and so did the other gentleman. He heard you a-calling from the path there, and run out in a hurry, and I looked out of the coffee-room window, but I didn't see you. 'Owever, he run off down the beach that way.'

Without a word we ran that way too – it was the opposite direction to that of last night's expedition. It wasn't quite four o'clock, and the day was fair, though not so fair as it had been, so that was really no reason, you'd say, for anxiety: with people about, surely a man couldn't come to much harm.

But something in our look as we ran out must have struck the servant, for she came out on the steps, and pointed, and said, 'Yes, that's the way he went.' We ran on as far as the top of the shingle bank, and there pulled up. There was a choice of ways: past the houses on the sea-front, or along the sand at the bottom of the beach, which, the tide being now out, was fairly broad. Or of course we might keep along the shingle between these two tracks and have some view of both of them; only that was heavy going. We chose the sand, for that was the loneliest, and someone might come to harm there without being seen from the public path.

Long said he saw Paxton some distance ahead, running and waving his stick, as if he wanted to signal to people who were on ahead of him. I couldn't be sure: one of these sea-mists was coming up very quickly from the south. There was someone, that's all I could say. And there were tracks on the sand as of someone running who wore shoes; and there were other tracks made before those – for the shoes sometimes trod in them and interfered with them – of someone not in shoes. Oh, of course, it's only my word you've got to take for all this: Long's dead, we'd no time or means to make sketches or take casts, and the next tide washed everything away. All we could do was to notice these marks as we hurried on. But there they were over and over again, and we had no doubt whatever that what we saw was the track of a bare foot, and one that showed more bones than flesh.

The notion of Paxton running after – after anything like this, and supposing it to be the friends he was looking for, was very dreadful to us. You can guess what we fancied: how the thing he was following might stop suddenly and turn round on him, and what sort of face it would show, half-seen at first in the mist – which all the while was getting thicker and thicker. And as I ran on wondering how the poor wretch could have been lured into mistaking that other thing for us, I remembered his saying, 'He has some power over your eyes.' And then I wondered what the end would be, for I had no hope now that the end could be averted, and – well, there is no need to tell all the dismal and horrid thoughts that flitted through my head as we ran on into the mist. It was uncanny, too, that the sun should still be bright in the sky and we could see nothing. We could only tell that we were now past the houses and had reached that gap there is between them and the old martello tower. When you are past the tower, you know, there is nothing but shingle for a long way – not a house, not a human creature; just that spit of land, or rather shingle, with the river on your right and the sea on your left.

But just before that, just by the martello tower, you remember there is the old battery, close to the sea. I believe there are only a few blocks of concrete left now: the rest has all been washed away, but at this time there was a lot more, though the place was a ruin. Well, when we got there, we clambered to the top as quick as we could to take breath and look over the shingle in front if by chance the mist would let us see anything. But a moment's rest we must have. We had run a mile at least. Nothing whatever was visible ahead of us, and we were just turning by common consent to get down and run hopelessly on, when we heard what I can only call a laugh: and if you can understand what I mean by a breathless, a lungless laugh, you have it: but I don't suppose you can. It came from below, and swerved away into the mist. That was enough. We bent over the wall. Paxton was there at the bottom.

You don't need to be told that he was dead. His tracks showed that he had run along the side of the battery, had turned sharp round the corner of it, and, small doubt of it, must have dashed straight into the open arms of someone who was waiting there. His mouth was full of sand and stones, and his teeth and jaws were broken to bits. I only glanced once at his face.

At the same moment, just as we were scrambling down from the battery to get to the body, we heard a shout, and saw a man running down the bank of the martello tower. He was the caretaker stationed there, and his keen old eyes had managed to descry through the mist that something was wrong. He had seen Paxton fall, and had seen us a moment after, running up – fortunate this, for otherwise we could hardly have escaped suspicion of being concerned in the dreadful business. Had he, we asked, caught sight of anybody attacking our friend? He could not be sure.

We sent him off for help, and stayed by the dead man till they came with the stretcher. It was then that we traced out how he had come, on the narrow fringe of sand under the battery wall. The rest was shingle, and it was hopelessly impossible to tell whither the other had gone.

What were we to say at the inquest? It was a duty, we felt, not to give up, there and then, the secret of the crown, to be published in every paper. I don't know how much you would have told; but what we did agree upon was this: to say that we had only made acquaintance with Paxton the day before, and that he had told us he was under some apprehension of danger at the hands of a man called William Ager. Also that we had seen some other tracks besides Paxton's when we followed him along the beach. But of course by that time everything was gone from the sands.

No one had any knowledge, fortunately, of any William Ager living in the district. The evidence of the man at the martello tower freed us from all suspicion. All that could be done was to return a verdict of wilful murder by some person or persons unknown.

Paxton was so totally without connections that all the inquiries that were subsequently made ended in a No Thoroughfare. And I have never been at Seaburgh, or even near it, since.

Edgar Allan Poe – The Masque of the Red Death

The "Red Death" had long devastated the country. No pestilence had ever been so fatal, or so hideous. Blood was its Avatar and its seal – the redness and the horror of blood. There were sharp pains, and sudden dizziness, and then profuse bleeding at the pores, with dissolution. The scarlet stains upon the body and especially upon the face of the victim, were the pest ban which shut him out from the aid and from the sympathy of his fellow-men. And the whole seizure, progress and termination of the disease, were the incidents of half an hour.

But the Prince Prospero was happy and dauntless and sagacious. When his dominions were half depopulated, he summoned to his presence a thousand hale and light-hearted friends from among the knights and dames of his court, and with these retired to the deep seclusion of one of his castellated abbeys. This was an extensive and magnificent structure, the creation of the prince's own eccentric yet august taste. A strong and lofty wall girdled it in. This wall had gates of iron. The courtiers, having entered, brought furnaces and massy hammers and welded the bolts. They resolved to leave means neither of ingress nor egress to the sudden impulses of despair or of frenzy from within. The abbey was amply provisioned. With such precautions the courtiers might bid defiance to contagion. The external world could take care of itself. In the meantime it was folly to grieve, or to think. The prince had provided all the appliances of pleasure. There were buffoons, there were improvisatori, there were ballet-dancers, there were musicians, there was Beauty, there was wine. All these and security were within. Without was the "Red Death".

It was towards the close of the fifth or sixth month of his seclusion, and while the pestilence raged most furiously abroad, that the Prince Prospero entertained his thousand friends at a masked ball of the most unusual magnificence.

It was a voluptuous scene, that masquerade. But first let me tell of the rooms in which it was held. These were seven – an imperial suite. In many palaces, however, such suites form a long and straight vista, while the folding doors slide back nearly to the walls on either hand, so that the view of the whole extent is scarcely impeded. Here the case was very different, as might have been expected from the duke's love of the *bizarre*. The apartments were so irregularly disposed that the vision embraced but little more than one at a time. There was a sharp turn at every twenty or thirty yards, and at each turn a novel effect. To the right and left, in the middle of each wall, a tall and narrow Gothic window looked out upon a closed corridor which pursued the windings of the suite. These windows were of stained glass whose colour varied in accordance with the prevailing hue of the decorations of the chamber into which it opened. That at the eastern extremity was hung, for example in blue – and vividly blue were its windows. The second chamber was purple in its ornaments and tapestries, and here the panes were purple. The third was green throughout, and so were the casements. The fourth was furnished and lighted with orange – the fifth with white – the sixth with violet. The seventh apartment was closely shrouded in black velvet tapestries that hung all over the ceiling and down the walls, falling in heavy folds upon a carpet of the same material and hue. But in this chamber only, the colour of the windows failed to correspond with the decorations. The panes here were scarlet – a deep blood colour. Now in no one of the seven apartments was there any lamp or candelabrum, amid the profusion of golden ornaments that lay scattered to and fro or depended from the roof. There was no light of any kind emanating from lamp or candle within the suite of chambers. But in the corridors that followed the suite, there stood, opposite to each window, a heavy tripod, bearing a brazier of fire, that projected its rays through the tinted glass and so glaringly illumined the room. And thus were produced a multitude of gaudy and fantastic appearances. But in the western or black chamber the effect of the fire-light that streamed upon the dark hangings through the blood-tinted panes, was ghastly in the extreme, and produced so wild a look upon the countenances of those who entered, that there were few of the company bold enough to set foot within its precincts at all.

It was in this apartment, also, that there stood against the western wall, a gigantic clock of ebony. Its pendulum swung to and fro with a dull, heavy, monotonous clang; and when the minute-hand made the circuit of the face, and the hour was to be stricken, there came from the brazen lungs of the clock a sound which was clear and loud and deep and exceedingly musical, but of so peculiar a note and emphasis that, at each lapse of an hour, the musicians of the orchestra were constrained to pause, momentarily, in their performance, to harken to the sound; and thus the waltzers perforce ceased their evolutions; and there was a brief disconcert of the whole gay company; and, while the chimes of the clock yet rang, it was observed that the giddiest grew pale, and the more aged and sedate passed their hands over their brows as if in confused revery or meditation. But when the echoes had fully ceased, a light laughter at once pervaded the assembly; the musicians looked at each other and smiled as if at their own nervousness and folly, and made whispering vows, each to the other, that the next chiming of the clock should produce in them no similar emotion; and then, after the lapse of sixty minutes (which embrace three thousand and six hundred seconds of the Time that flies), there came yet another chiming of the clock, and then were the same disconcert and tremulousness and meditation as before.

But, in spite of these things, it was a gay and magnificent revel. The tastes of the duke were peculiar. He had a fine eye for colours and effects. He disregarded the *decora* of mere fashion. His plans were bold and fiery, and his conceptions glowed with barbaric lustre. There are some who would have thought him mad. His followers felt that he was not. It was necessary to hear and see and touch him to be *sure* that he was not.

He had directed, in great part, the movable embellishments of the seven chambers, upon occasion of this great *fête*; and it was his own guiding taste which had given character to the masqueraders. Be sure they were grotesque. There were much glare and glitter and piquancy and phantasm – much of what has been since seen in "Hernani". There were arabesque figures with unsuited limbs and appointments. There were delirious fancies such as the madman fashions. There were much of the beautiful, much of the wanton, much of the *bizarre*, something of the terrible, and not a little of that which might have excited disgust. To and fro in the seven chambers there stalked, in fact, a multitude of dreams. And these – the dreams – writhed in and about taking hue from the rooms, and causing the wild music of the orchestra to seem as the echo of their steps. And, anon, there strikes the ebony clock which stands in the hall of the velvet. And then, for a moment, all is still, and all is silent save the voice of the clock. The dreams are stiff-frozen as they stand. But the echoes of the chime die away – they have endured but an instant – and a light, half-subdued laughter floats after them as they depart. And now again the music swells, and the dreams live, and writhe to and fro more merrily than ever, taking hue from the many tinted windows through which stream the rays from the tripods. But to the chamber which lies most westwardly of the seven, there are now none of the maskers who venture; for the night is waning away; and there flows a ruddier light through the blood-coloured panes; and the blackness of the sable drapery appals; and to him whose foot falls upon the sable carpet, there comes from the near clock of ebony a muffled peal more solemnly emphatic than any which reaches *their* ears who indulged in the more remote gaieties of the other apartments.

But these other apartments were densely crowded, and in them beat feverishly the heart of life. And the revel went whirlingly on, until at length there commenced the sounding of midnight upon the clock. And then the music ceased, as I have told; and the evolutions of the waltzers were quieted; and there was an uneasy cessation of all things as before. But now there were twelve strokes to be sounded by the bell of the clock; and thus it happened, perhaps, that more of thought crept, with more of time, into the meditations of the thoughtful among those who revelled. And thus too, it happened, perhaps, that before the last echoes of the last chime had utterly sunk into silence, there were many individuals in the crowd who had found leisure to become aware of the presence of a masked figure which had arrested the attention of no single individual before. And the rumour of this new presence having spread itself whisperingly around, there arose at length from the whole company a buzz, or murmur, expressive of disapprobation and surprise – then, finally, of terror, of horror, and of disgust.

In an assembly of phantasms such as I have painted, it may well be supposed that no ordinary appearance could have excited such sensation. In truth the masquerade licence of the night was nearly unlimited; but the figure in question had out-Heroded Herod, and gone beyond the bounds of even the prince's indefinite decorum. There are chords in the hearts of the most reckless which cannot be touched without emotion. Even with the utterly lost, to whom life and death are equally jests, there are matters of which no jest can be made. The whole company, indeed, seemed now deeply to feel that in the costume and bearing of the stranger neither wit nor propriety existed. The figure was tall and gaunt, and shrouded from head to foot in the habiliments of the grave. The mask which concealed the visage was made so nearly to resemble the countenance of a stiffened corpse that the closest scrutiny must have had difficulty in detecting the cheat. And yet all this might have been endured, if not approved, by the mad revellers around. But the mummer had gone so far as

216

to assume the type of the Red Death. His vesture was dabbled in *blood* – and his broad brow, with all the features of the face, was besprinkled with the scarlet horror.

When the eyes of the Prince Prospero fell upon this spectral image (which, with a slow and solemn movement, as if more fully to sustain its role, stalked to and fro among the waltzers) he was seen to be convulsed, in the first moment with a strong shudder either of terror or distaste; but, in the next, his brow reddened with rage.

"Who dares," – he demanded hoarsely of the courtiers who stood near him – "who dares insult us with this blasphemous mockery? Seize him and unmask him – that we may know whom we have to hang, at sunrise, from the battlements!"

It was in the eastern or blue chamber in which stood the Prince Prospero as he uttered these words. They rang throughout the seven rooms loudly and clearly, for the prince was a bold and robust man, and the music had become hushed at the waving of his hand.

It was in the blue room where stood the prince, with a group of pale courtiers by his side. At first, as he spoke, there was a slight rushing movement of this group in the direction of the intruder, who at the moment was also near at hand, and now, with deliberate and stately step, made closer approach to the speaker. But from a certain nameless awe with which the mad assumptions of the mummer had inspired the whole party, there were found none who put forth hand to seize him; so that, unimpeded, he passed within a yard of the prince's person; and, while the vast assembly, as if with one impulse, shrank from the centres of the rooms to the walls, he made his way uninterruptedly, but with the same solemn and measured step which had distinguished him from the first, through the blue chamber to the purple – through the purple to the green – through the green to the orange – through this again to the white – and even thence to the violet, ere a decided movement had been made to arrest him. It was then, however, that the Prince Prospero, maddening with rage and the shame of his own momentary cowardice, rushed hurriedly through the six chambers, while none followed him on account of a deadly terror that had seized upon all. He bore aloft a drawn dagger, and had approached, in rapid impetuosity, to within three or four feet of the retreating figure, when the latter, having attained the extremity of the velvet apartment, turned suddenly and confronted his pursuer. There was a sharp cry – and the dagger dropped gleaming upon the sable carpet, upon which, instantly afterwards, fell prostrate in death the Prince Prospero. Then, summoning the wild courage of despair, a throng of the revellers at once threw themselves into the black apartment, and, seizing the mummer, whose tall figure stood erect and motionless within the shadow of the ebony clock, gasped in unutterable horror at finding the grave cerements and corpse-like mask, which they handled with so violent a rudeness, untenanted by any tangible form.

And now was acknowledged the presence of the Red Death. He had come like a thief in the night. And one by one dropped the revellers in the blood-bedewed halls of their revel, and died each in the despairing posture of his fall. And the life of the ebony clock went out with that of the last of the gay. And the flames of the tripods expired. And Darkness and Decay and the Red Death held illimitable dominion over all.